Praise for *Bridge of D*

"Gwendolyn Greene and the Moondog Coronation Ball of 1957" is excellent, as I expected. It reminded me of everything I loved about *The Captive Condition*. Much like Donald Ray Pollock's stories, it churns on its own weird, relentless engine. I particularly like the rhythm and economy of language throughout.
James Renner, author of *Little, Crazy Children*

Layer upon layer, world upon world, Kevin P. Keating has created a thriving ecosystem of stories. From the past to the future to the dark corners of our mind, Keating's writing weaves myths and genres into a fully realized world just a few delightful degrees off of our own. A world — built on smart, at times exhilarating writing — I only wished I could spend a few more hours in.
Noah Sanders, editor of *The Racket Journal*

A serpentine, mysterious book, *Bridge of Dreams* spans three wild stories of UFOs, pioneer heroes, and the flickering nature of someone standing right before you. And that is just the surface of a larger romance that winds its way through fantastic treehouses, caves of horror, and the secret destiny of the girl next door's really good dog. More of a maze than a bridge, it is one you begin tracing with your finger instead of a pencil because you don't want to commit yourself to only one way out as you inevitably — and gleefully — start over again. A transporting, weird adventure across time, space, and the shimmering surface of reality itself, Keating's masterful ability to two-step across multiple genres puts *Bridge of Dreams* squarely in the tradition of Hawthorne in that, no matter what the cover says, there will be a part of you that will think this is true.
Brad Ricca, author of *Mrs. Sherlock Holmes*

"Gwendolyn Greene and the Moondog Coronation Ball of 1957" is a fantastic novella that blends heartwarming hometown interaction with elements of science fiction. As a dog-lover (I have two), I appreciated the bond Gwendolyn had with her pooch, and the relationship between them, as depicted by Gwendolyn's nameless childhood friend, felt so honest and real. And let's take a moment to applaud the author's bravery in giving us a narrator who isn't named. It's an interesting choice that lends a compelling sense of "otherness" to what is ultimately a small-town tale.

Melissa A. Bartell, editor of *Bibliotica*

Bridge of Dreams

A Speculative Triptych

Other Books by Kevin P. Keating

The Natural Order of Things 978-0804169271
The Captive Condition 978-0804169288

Bridge of Dreams

A Speculative Triptych

Kevin P. Keating

IFF
BOOKS

London, UK
Washington, DC, USA

CollectiveInk

First published by iff Books, 2025
iff Books is an imprint of Collective Ink Ltd.,
Unit 11, Shepperton House, 89 Shepperton Road, London, N1 3DF
office@collectiveinkbooks.com
www.collectiveinkbooks.com
www.iff-books.com

For distributor details and how to order please visit the 'Ordering' section on our website.

ISBN: 978 1 80341 803 2
978 1 80341 811 7 (ebook)
Library of Congress Control Number: 2024933333

A CIP catalogue record for this book is available from the British Library.

Design: Lapiz Digital Services

UK: Printed and bound by CPI Group (UK) Ltd, Croydon, CR0 4YY
Printed in North America by CPI GPS partners

We operate a distinctive and ethical publishing philosophy in all areas of our business, from our global network of authors to production and worldwide distribution.

Contents

For Rose

It's unnecessary to introduce magic into the explanation of physical and biological phenomenon when, in fact, there's every likelihood that the continuation of research, as it's now practiced, will indeed fill in all the gaps.

Sir John Maddox, denouncing the work of Rupert Sheldrake

Acknowledgments

Like most works of fiction, this novel evolved over a period of several years and went through extensive revision. I am indebted to those who graciously read, commented on, edited, and published excerpts of *Bridge of Dreams* as it was slowly taking shape. I am particularly grateful to Mike Pickett, editor of *Lost Colony Magazine*, who was the first to champion the story of Gwendolyn Greene and her intrepid dog McKenna. Other literary journals that published early drafts of these pages include *The Racket, Et Sequitur, Belle Ombre, The Nonconformist, White Wall Review, Aji, Potato Soup, Toasted Cheese, Better Than Starbucks, The Mark,* and *Crossways Literary Journal*.

Writers, continually racked by self-doubt, sometimes find themselves flying solo with no one to believe in their idiosyncratic and farfetched ideas, but with *Bridge of Dreams* I was incredibly fortunate to have the encouragement, guidance, and advocacy of my daughter Rose. She inspired me to dream up this fantastical, fictitious world, and contributed to the final product by reading draft after draft, pointing out errors and offering suggestions for improvement. This book exists largely thanks to her.

Foreword

Much has been said about subverting audience or reader expectations, and much of what is said about it seems to treat it as a virtue in and of itself. If the book or movie subverts expectations, that automatically makes it a better book or movie. I couldn't disagree more. Subverting expectations is a tool in the storyteller's toolbox, but the mere fact that the storyteller uses it doesn't necessarily make the story good. What matters is what it is used for. When a storyteller subverts expectations merely by taking away what the audience expected, it is the narrative equivalent of pulling a chair out from under someone as they are about to sit in it. It's sure to get a reaction, but it's not nearly as clever as the prankster thinks it is. The trick about subverting expectations is that the storyteller needs to take away what the audience was expecting and give them something better in its place.

Bridge of Dreams sets up the narrator as the classic hero. He rides off to Cleveland to save Gwendolyn and McKenna from the Moondog Coronation Ball like Luke Skywalker going to rescue Princess Leia from the Death Star's detention level. And he seems to be on the verge of success, but just then, he's stopped. Disaster strikes. If the story ended there, I would put it closer to the "pulling the chair out" trick, but it doesn't end there. The story continues and what we get instead of a classic hero's story is a thoughtful rumination on regret, missed chances, grief, and transcendence. What does it mean if we failed to seize on our chance to do something truly great? Would success have drastically changed the trajectory of our lives? Was there ever really a chance that the outcome could have been different? Or is life really about finding some meaning in all of the random events that happen around us, events that we don't have as much control over as we like to think that we do?

Bridge of Dreams raises all of these questions because it doesn't give us the classic hero's ending that it seems to be setting us up for. My favorite stories give me something to think about after I've finished reading. They usually leave me with more questions than answers. *Bridge of Dreams* does that for me. I hope it does the same for you, too.

M.E. Pickett, editor and publisher of *Lost Colony Magazine*

Introduction

Due to the unprecedented success of the first edition of "Gwendolyn Greene and the Moondog Coronation Ball of 1957" (Lost Colony Press), my new publisher has decided, after a little late-night cajoling and some excruciating aesthetic compromises on the part of its author, to issue this corrected and greatly expanded second edition. In the spring of 2023, during my coast-to-coast book tour, I made your acquaintance, Diligent Reader, in crowded conference halls, noisy seminar rooms, and rowdy college taverns. While signing books, I had the pleasure of listening to your own stories. I have this gift, you see, for drawing people in, particularly unscrupulous middle managers, shady criminal lawyers, and kleptocratic city council members who feel a burning need to brag about their corruption and incompetence. With all the genteel scheming among the professional classes, I've never lacked good material — or an embarrassing confrontation or two.

Here I must pause to extend my heartfelt apologies to the bartender in Peebles, Ohio (home of the prestigious Serpent Mound Literary Festival) who sustained a few minor injuries (twisted left ankle, bruised right knee, an unsightly case of cauliflower ear) when a famously petulant, blue-blooded, baby-faced critic, under the influence of something far more exotic than the watered-down rum punch we were sipping in celebration of my novella's release, elbowed his way to my strategically placed corner stool and yanked from the eager hands of an aspiring SF writer a signed copy of my novella, the wet ink from my fountain pen fanning across the title page. Launching into a semi-coherent tirade ("Jupiter D rockets! Jupiter D! Are you mad? Do a little research, you hack! And Laika reached earth

orbit in early November, not December, you baldheaded buffoon!"),
this deeply disturbed individual fumbled in his shirt pocket for a
box of matches ("Ideal for the home smoker," the label guaranteed),
ceremonially turned to Chapter 13 (a reliable fan favorite), and then
attempted to set my book ablaze. To my relief, he couldn't control his
shaking hands long enough to strike a match. The bartender, a burly
cornfed brute with a busted nose and a pair of bloodshot eyes, escorted
the would-be arsonist to the back alley where, I'm told, he taught
him an unforgettable lesson in literary citizenship. Meanwhile, the
apprentice SF writer, rather than ask for a new copy, pressed the
book to her chest and said she planned to have my smeared signature
framed and mounted on her apartment wall. "Won't the other Dog-
Eared Detectives be jealous," she said with a backward sashay and
enigmatic grin. "Our book club. Meets every other Wednesday. Seven
o'clock sharp. Arthurian Estates. Ask for Heloise at the gate."

There were a few notable incidents and accidents elsewhere
(accusations of card counting at a blackjack table in Mesquite, Nevada;
man overboard during a moonlight barge party on the Cuyahoga
River), but these scenes I took to be good omens. Show me an author
who doesn't crave a little notoriety at the start of a national tour. And
I never became so distracted as to ignore completely your suggestions
for revision. A fair number of you requested a word or two about
our famously roguish editor. While such a Falstaffian figure would
doubtless make for an amusing read, I've decided the scintillating wit
of Magistrate Mike, as the public has fondly come to know him, must
wait until the twenty-fifth-anniversary edition of this book, that is, if
my publisher's doors remain open and the continued popularity of my
work warrants one. The indignities and hardships of the book trade!

In the preface to the first edition, I briefly described what inspired
me to write such an idiosyncratic but essential history of the space race.
I incorrectly assumed that my readers would show little patience for
my melodramatic flair, but now, having listened to your enthusiastic
demands for more legends about Heavenly Hill, I've reconsidered my
position. For this expanded edition, I've composed two new novellas,

2

"Hilda Whitby and the Heavenly Light of 1857" and "IMPETUS 13 and the Constitutional Crisis of 2057." Together with "Gwendolyn," this trio of stories comprises one unified narrative, what I have chosen to call a speculative triptych. My editorial team was then faced with a crucial decision. In which order should the novellas appear? Should "Gwendolyn" lead the pack as initially planned? Or would it be better to take a more conventional approach and begin with "Hilda," the story that chronologically comes first? Or might the book benefit from a more avant-garde approach by starting in the year 2057 and introducing readers to the new and improved IMPETUS 13™?

My daughter and part-time editorial assistant, when not maniacally laughing at online doggy videos or dusting her collection of vintage dolls in the attic, told me the decision was not mine to make.

"Once the book is out in the wild," she said during teatime with her three dearest dolls, Maggie, Hilda, and Gwendolyn, "the author relinquishes control. For all you know, some people may choose to read the entire thing from back to front. It all depends on the kind of experience they want to have. Isn't that so, Maggie?" She held a tiny teacup to a doll's unsmiling lips. "What, too much sugar? Then why did you ask for three lumps instead of your usual two?"

With the tea party threatening to spiral out of control, I left my assistant's room and retreated to my study, where, for the next few hours, I pondered her sage advice. She was right. I needed to trust my readers. They were perfectly capable of deciding for themselves how to read this book. And if anything seemed unclear, they could always annotate, underscore, and highlight the thorny passages and then return to them after finishing the entire thing. Hell, for all I cared, they could draw pictures and diagrams in the margins if it helped them navigate my little linguistic labyrinth.

Still, a decision had to be made. The book was going to press in one week.

While sitting at my desk, I drew names from a SpaceCamp ball cap, and this, Diligent Reader, is the order in which I present these stories to you now. In many ways, I'm pleased with the way chance decided the outcome. In the edition you currently hold in your hands, "Gwendolyn" appears first. Her story serves as a prelude that introduces and develops many of the book's central themes. Since so many of you are already well-acquainted with the plot and characters, my hope is that it will be like hearing a familiar melody in a concerto's opening movement. "Hilda" comes next, serving as a kind of way station and expanding upon ideas hinted at in earlier chapters. "IMPETUS 13" works as a finale in which each of the book's themes is quietly but emphatically restated, providing no easy resolutions and inviting readers to reconsider everything that has come before. The overarching narrative scheme works best in this order, but then what do I know?

Beleaguered composition instructor by necessity, reluctant raconteur by request, and writer by sheer compulsion, I take the position that a book, like its author, should have several identities and be read in different ways. I realize, of course, that paying customers on the hunt for a quality novel at an affordable price have certain expectations for how a story ought to unfold. I'm referring not only to timing, tone, and tantalizing plot twists but to structure. A predictable sequence of images. A map to guide the way. Lately, however, I've grown tired of using the same time-tested techniques and have started experimenting with form. Since the reader-author relationship is usually a reciprocal one, I assume many of you will understand what I'm trying to say. But to be clear, you may tackle these stories in any order you choose. I leave the decision entirely up to you.

Kevin P. Keating
Visiting Lecturer
Center for Advanced Consciousness Studies
Aspern College

First Trip

Gwendolyn Greene and the Moondog
Coronation Ball of 1957

One

On a dusty country lane, leaning toward an otherwise unremarkable farmhouse of indeterminate age, stands a solitary historical marker that, at least in theory, is meant to attract the attention of passing motorists. With its easily forgotten names and dates, the marker may vanish one day beneath a sea of tall grass, and no one will be any the wiser, including some of the committee members who helped raise the funds to have it placed there. If, by chance, a few lost travelers trying to find their way back to the interstate after a day of antiquing in town or a weekend of camping in the nearby state park, do stop to read the succinct paragraph inscribed on its bronze plaque, they will learn of a girl who, many years ago, lived in this house and made a small contribution to human progress, though I'm not sure she would have appreciated my use of the word "progress."

For a time, the committee considered purchasing the property from its current occupants and converting the house into a museum, but Heavenly Hill, situated in a remote rural corner of the state, would never attract enough visitors to warrant even relatively modest restoration costs. Still, the members unanimously agreed that something needed to be done to keep Gwendolyn Margaret Greene's memory alive. During her short life, she never craved recognition, and I'm doubtful she would have wanted a historical marker drawing attention to her childhood home. In time, she came to value privacy. During our final conversation, she also told me that trivial facts had nothing to do with reality because they failed to tell a meaningful story. For this reason alone, Gwendolyn disliked history, or maybe I should say *distrusted* it. She lived in her head a lot of the time, certainly much more than I ever did, and she could be strident in her views.

The house sits half an acre from the road on a hill overlooking Lost Village Lake. Like so many of the homes in Heavenly Hill, this one needs a fresh coat of paint, new windows, gutters, roof, and masonry work. The foundation's handmade bricks have started to buckle and crumble, and whenever a ferocious summer storm sweeps over the lake, the tiles peel from the rooftop and sail into the weeds and wildflowers. In 1957, when Gwendolyn lived here, the house had been in slightly better condition. Her mother, suffering from a chronic case of dysmetropsia, had died three years earlier when, rather than shrink and tumble head over heels into the sky, she hit her head on the family dock and fell unconscious into the lake.

After the tragedy, Gwendolyn took over most of the household chores. She tried keeping the place tidy. She hung linens on the clothesline, scrubbed the kitchen countertops and floors, and set traps in the cellar to catch the mice that nested behind the boiler. She never complained and never spoke ill of her father.

The first farmer in our county to raise alpacas ("Dumber than deer," he used to gripe, "dumber than goats"), Mr. Enoch Greene had started drinking too much. A once ambitious but largely unsuccessful man, he often grew wistful and made his daughter empty promises: "I'll build you a treehouse one day, my princess. An enchanted castle for you and your retinue where all of your dreams come true." He fell asleep in the barn after working long hours in the pens. Gwendolyn found him half-buried in the haystacks, surrounded by empty whisky bottles and bleating alpacas. With their long necks and inquisitive child-like eyes, the animals looked like extraterrestrials, and Gwendolyn sometimes wondered while standing in a ring of lantern light if they were castaways abandoned centuries ago by the mothership. A notion I now take seriously. I recently read somewhere that on the high arid plateaus of the Peruvian Andes, there are mysterious temple ruins and enormous animal geoglyphs that heterodox astronomers believe to be sophisticated maps of the Milky Way.

Behind their house, on a gentle slope leading down the lake, stood the tallest, if not the oldest, tree in Heavenly Hill, its enormous limbs reaching like outstretched arms up to the heavens. While no one would describe him as a nature lover, Gwendolyn's father adored and took great pride in that white oak. Gazing over forests and fields for at least two centuries, the tree seemed to keep watch over their house, and perhaps Mr. Greene mistakenly believed it would shield his family from life's tragedies.

Father and daughter managed as best they could and seemed happy enough together. But about the late Mrs. Greene, neither one ever uttered a word.

Two

As Gwendolyn's last surviving childhood friend and as the publisher of Heavenly Hill's weekly newsletter, *The Sentinel* (to call it a newspaper would be farcical), I was invited by the committee to compose a first draft of the historical marker. There were five members in all — the assistant librarian, the junior high math teacher, the retired city councilwoman, the orthodontist's wife, always quick to remind the rest of us of her generosity in providing most of the funds for the project, and the eccentric pensioner who, at a makeshift desk in his one-room cabin overlooking the lake, wrote a newsletter that he photocopied at his own expense and distributed to a handful of small businesses along Main Street.

History as a collective effort is usually indistinguishable from propaganda, and it was only a short time before the committee insisted upon giving its editorial feedback and granting its final approval of what I'd written. Evidently, they'd expected me to compose something that could pass as socially sanctioned piety, but mainly they took issue with my depiction of Gwendolyn's Australian Shepherd McKenna as "an unscrupulous sneak with a long criminal record, a gray-eyed scoundrel with a taste for vanilla custard and whipped cream."

The offending quote, I pointed out, was taken directly from an old feature story by Willard Anderson, the longtime editor-in-chief of *The Sentinel*. Today, *The Sentinel* is just a hobby of mine, not an honest profession, but in the summer of 1957, Heavenly Hill's newspaper was a proper tabloid with a small staff of full-time reporters, copyeditors, ad men, and a chain-smoking, charmingly alcoholic editor who took the occasional liberty with his uninspiring source material. His motto: "A typewriter will invent any truth you choose." Willard Anderson ran stories about everything from the Red Scare to the latest bank auction of a family farm. Economic hardship and nuclear annihilation were his favorite themes. Almost every morning, paranoid readers were told that intercontinental ballistic missiles might at any moment rain down on their heads and lay waste to the free world. At the prospect of nuclear winter and national extinction, a few neighbors built bunkers behind their houses. Our science teacher, Mr. Watts, sent away for a short-wave radio and claimed to have heard the steady *beep-beep-beep* of a Russian satellite circling the globe.

"Sometimes," he said, "I fear the government is trying to transistorize our brains."

Whenever he sensed his overstimulated subscribers needed a laugh, Mr. Anderson published the occasional human-interest story. One such story has been preserved in the local library's digital archives. The 500-word feature includes a grainy black-and-white photo of a professionally groomed dog and can be easily accessed by the committee members if they have the inclination to read it, which they do not. Back in 1957, while awaiting the inevitable apocalypse and before turning to the crossword puzzle, amused readers skimmed the story before dismissing it as the fantasies of a man who'd penned it late at night after uncorking the ubiquitous bottle of bourbon stashed in his bottom desk drawer. But as an eyewitness to the events described, I can personally attest to the story's accuracy.

On a sweltering afternoon in late June, while sitting at his desk near the big picture window, Willard Anderson observed a petty crime down the street at the corner soda shop. Waving his hand through the haze of cigarette smoke that hung heavy over the newsroom, he leaned forward to get a better look at the local girl and her "canine bandit." Gwendolyn had gotten into the habit of taking McKenna for long walks into town and leaving him unattended outside the shop while she treated herself to a chocolate phosphate.

With a violent shake of his neck and quick twist of his head, McKenna slipped from his collar and performed tricks for the children sitting with their parents at the sidewalk tables. In the bright sunshine, he paced along the curb and balanced a tennis ball on his snout. After an enthusiastic round of applause, the children lowered their paper cups and gave him the sticky remnants of their vanilla custard. Unsatisfied with these meager offerings, McKenna devised a clever tactic for getting an entire ice cream cone, and it didn't take long before he saw an opportunity to score big. With a perfectly calibrated swing of his head, he tossed his ball to a group of toddlers milling around the soda shop. Sure enough, a little boy dropped his cone in a clumsy attempt to catch the ball. McKenna pounced. Within seconds, he wolfed down the sugar cone and strawberry custard splattered on the pavement.

Rather than howl at the injustice of his fate, the boy stood there, staring stupidly at the ground. His little sister was far more vigilant. Familiar now with the dog's antics, she jealously guarded her cone and ignored his invitations to play. McKenna tried giving her the sad eyes. When he realized this ploy wouldn't work on one so wise, he gave a loud snort of frustration, scratched his left ear, and trotted down the block. He waited for a customer to exit the five-and-dime and then darted inside the open door. A few minutes later, amid distant shouts, he returned with a large plastic pony hanging daintily from his teeth, the mare's luxurious blonde mane and tail sweeping against the sidewalk. The little girl beamed. McKenna placed the pony at her feet and ran his tongue over his slavering mouth. When the girl reached down to grab the pony, McKenna snatched the scoop of raspberry sorbet dripping from her cone and bounded away.

By then, Linus Lambert, proprietor of Lambert & Sons Resale Shop, stormed down the street. He fiddled with the oil-slicked strands of his combover, seized the pony from the girl, and demanded to know why "this mongrel" wasn't on its leash. When Gwendolyn stepped outside the soda shop, she immediately guessed what had happened. She sipped her phosphate and watched the girl burst into tears while McKenna, ears flat against his head, slunk away in shame.

But watching from his office window, feet propped on his desk, a fresh cigarette burning between his lips, Willard Anderson reported that the dog had "a triumphant swagger and on its face a sly smile that only a fellow crook could recognize."

Three

The following afternoon, having made a formal appointment over the phone, Willard Anderson arrived at the Greenes' house. McKenna, resting on the front stoop, seemed to have been expecting him and greeted the editor with a friendly yap of hello. Gwendolyn invited the editor to sit in one of the rocking chairs and instructed McKenna to fetch a beer for their guest. The dog darted down the steps and disappeared around back. When he returned, he had a cold can of Duke in his mouth, which he placed with care at Anderson's feet.

In 1957, when I first read the article, I wasn't sure why Gwendolyn had agreed to the interview and photoshoot. Maybe like a proud mother who can't help boasting about her talented child, she simply wanted to see McKenna's name in print. Only later, after the animal psychologists and rocket scientists descended on Heavenly Hill, did Gwendolyn confide that she and McKenna had made a secret pact to alter the course of history.

What follows is an excerpt from the article:

The charming Ms. Greene has been training the Australian Shepherd since he was a pup, and she takes great pride in his abilities — sit, shake, stay, fetch, roll over. Whenever he is hungry, he happily trots to the family's upright piano in the front parlor and pounds on the keys. But what's truly remarkable about this precocious pooch is his uncanny ability to comprehend human language. According to Ms. Greene, her dog understands nearly one thousand words.

Sensing my skepticism, she kindly offered to give me a demonstration and set about hiding a dozen toys around the yard.

"Find big baby!" she called out.

Panting with excitement, McKenna raced through the yard, sniffing around every bush and tree until he dragged an old rag doll from under a hedge.

"Find blue elephant!"

In no time McKenna spotted a stuffed animal tucked between the thick roots of an old oak.

"Find ball, stick, frisbee, hula hoop, sandal…"

The demonstration continued for the next thirty minutes, during which time, I'm happy to report, McKenna was also told to fetch more cans of cold beer.

Later, after saying goodbye to Ms. Greene, I realized I'd misplaced my car keys, not unusual for a man of my years. McKenna sprinted to the porch and found them wedged between the chair cushions. He raced back to me and placed the keyring in my hand. For a minute, I thought he might hop into the driver's seat, snap on the radio, and chauffeur me home while I listened to the ballgame. A more superstitious man might be tempted to say the dog possesses extrasensory perception.

For his part, Willard Anderson wasn't exactly guilty of journalistic malfeasance. Like everyone else, he simply assumed that Gwendolyn had trained the dog herself and never thought to ask if McKenna had come by his abilities in a more unusual way. No doubt, some will argue that what transpired weeks before on a starry night in early June had nothing to do with McKenna's gifts. They're probably correct. I have no wish to argue the point and no interpretation to offer. I only know that the dog's behavior became increasingly difficult to explain. Difficult to explain, that is, for those who only know part of the story.

Gwendolyn and I never told anyone about what transpired two weeks earlier, and decades would pass before we brought the subject up again in conversation. But by then, so many years had slipped away that it was difficult for us to make sense of what indeed *had* happened. My sole purpose in describing the incident is to unburden myself of the secret we kept for all these years, the details of which do not appear on the historical marker bearing Gwendolyn's name.

Four

During our first night of summer vacation, shortly before circumstances compelled her to leave Heavenly Hill and vanish into the anonymity of conventional suburban life, I had the privilege of rowing Gwendolyn in her father's skiff to the center of Lost Village Lake. One mile wide, three miles long, and reaching depths of more than one hundred fifty feet, the lake was, in fact, a reservoir created during the Great Depression when the state built a hydroelectric dam and flooded the valley. Before that, an old canal ran the valley's length, passing through the ruins of a frontier town with a saloon notorious for its carnivals of sin and violence, and a renegade church whose female pastor was recognized by no denomination. According to legend, the Reverend Hilda Whitby could see into the past and future, and her wraith-like appearance silenced even her most impassioned detractors.

Local fishermen said that on still nights like this, if a gibbous moon was shining at just the right angle and your boat didn't make a ripple on the water, you could peer over the gunnel and see a cluster of frame buildings in the murky depths, the peaks of their submerged rooftops visible above swaying tendrils of seaweed; and if you were very quiet and the loons weren't calling, you could sometimes hear Hilda lambasting her quaking congregants, her ghostly whisper bubbling up from a drowned world.

I'd always felt Gwendolyn had some mysterious connection to the lake and could summon the spirit of the preacher woman, but on this particular night, she was preoccupied with the present, not the past.

As we approached the center of the lake, she gave me the signal to raise the oars and said, "Perfect spot to conduct our ecological experiment."

McKenna, napping at the bow, cracked open an eye and watched the geese fly in formation above the moonlit lake. He yawned, adjusted his head against the bench, and let the gentle waves rock him back to sleep.

Gwendolyn reached into the leather satchel at her feet and produced two mason jars. Inside were dozens of tiny mollusks, their shells zigzagged with black and white stripes.

"Zebra mussels," she said.

"Wait a second," I said. "Where'd you get those?"

"You know where," she answered. "They're stowaways. From the Caspian Sea. Hitched a ride in the ballast tank of a cargo ship until they reached Lake Erie. An invasive species, that's what Mr. Watts called them."

"Did you take those from the science lab?"

"I rescued them. It had to be done. Mr. Watts might leave them to die over the summer. You know how forgetful he can be." She tapped one of the jars and held it up to catch a little starlight. "I think they'll filter out animal waste and contamination from farm runoff. But he insists they'll colonize the lake bottom. What did he tell us in class? 'They'll consume vast quantities of algae. Starve the lake of its nutrients. Upset the freshwater ecosystem.'"

Gwendolyn was a great mimic, and I laughed at her impersonation of our teacher's nasally British accent. A former schoolmaster from Kent, Abelard Watts told us how he'd taught his pupils in the Chislehurst Caves, where dozens of families had taken refuge from daily German bombardments. A man of cool, analytical intelligence. A good teacher. A kind human being. I miss him terribly.

"What do you plan to do with those things?" I asked.

Gwendolyn smiled in that maddening way of hers and twisted open a lid.

"Let's see who's right. Me or Mr. Watts."

I looked over my shoulder, half-expecting to see our science teacher glaring at us from the water's edge. During the week, Mr. Watts taught biology, chemistry, and physics at Heavenly Hill High. On the weekends, he served as our city council president and moderated a bible study group at Book Your Trip, the little novelty shop and used bookstore on the square. Friday evenings, he took long strolls along the lake and contemplated topics for that weekend's discussion: Dante, Virgil, and an obsessive preoccupation with personal immortality. In a small town like ours, people were obliged to wear many hats.

Now, in an oddly ceremonial fashion, Gwendolyn lifted a jar above her head and dumped its contents into the lake. I watched the shells spiral counterclockwise into the inky darkness, wondering how long it would take before the mussels did their work. Gwendolyn may have been the brightest girl in our class, and with her long auburn hair and big blue eyes also the prettiest, but she could be confident to the point of recklessness. She resisted the slightest encroachment on her sovereignty by the rest of society, and humility before Nature was something she had yet to learn.

Decades after conducting her so-called experiment, the reservoir has gradually gone from a chalky gray to the icy blue of a glacial lake in the Swiss Alps. Today, no matter the season, but especially in the fall when the leaves change colors, the water so vividly mirrors the sky and surrounding landscape that visitors sometimes feel as though they're falling into the clouds. The lake is also so deprived of algae and nutrients, as Mr. Watts predicted, that the bluegill and largemouth bass that once thrived here no longer inhabit its waters.

Gwendolyn was about to open the second jar when McKenna, whimpering in his sleep, jumped to his feet. He began to pace around our small skiff, his nails clattering against the creaking bottom boards.

"McKenna!" Gwendolyn cried, gripping the sides of the boat as it rocked back and forth. "What are you *doing*? You have a bad dream or something?"

The dog abruptly stood at attention and stared at the horizon. "What is it, boy? You want to go home already?"

Gwendolyn scratched his neck and then reached for a second jar. This time, instead of dumping the contents, she let the mussels fall one by one into the lake. We listened to the alternating plops and silence, and watched the ripples spread across the water. McKenna, still staring at the sky, began to growl.

"Oh, that's enough now," Gwendolyn said. "Tell me what's wrong?"

McKenna pressed against her legs and barked. The hemlock stirred in a sudden rush of cold air. A blue heron tiptoeing through the cattails on the far shore took wing. Warblers exploded from the reeds. Then, an eerie stillness settled over everything. I turned with a shrug to Gwendolyn. Her face began to glow an incandescent green and vanished altogether in a white light so radiant that I had to turn away and cover my eyes with one arm. An instant later, I heard a sonic boom and felt a shower of cinders. There was a shriek and a monstrous splash that nearly capsized us. I reached out for Gwendolyn and almost tumbled into the whitecaps that threatened to swamp us, their crests touched by a spectral light.

Feeling slightly seasick, I sat on the bench and waited for the waves to subside.

McKenna, now curled tightly at her feet, looked at Gwendolyn and whined.

"Nearly vaporized us," she whispered, stroking his head.

She tapped me with her shoe and snapped her fingers. "Well? Come on. Pick up those oars. Let's check it out."

Something told me to turn around and head back to shore, but I was more frightened of disobeying my captain's order.

I thrust the oars into the water and began to row, only this time I had to put my back and shoulders into it. The bow cut sharply through the waves, and when we reached the spot where the thing touched down, I slumped over on the bench. Except for my panting and the hooting of a horned owl, all was quiet.

Gwendolyn pointed.

"Look!"

Half-expecting to hear the steady hiss of steam rising from the water, I craned over the side and detected a faint greenish glow beneath the surface. As if pulled by the force of a swirling vortex, our boat started to rotate slowly around the fading light.

"What do you suppose it could be?" I breathed.

"A meteorite?" she said. "A hunk of magnesium, judging from the color. Those things are known to travel for millions of years through outer space. Or it might be debris. From a spacecraft. Miles told me the Soviets are developing rockets that can reach orbit before disintegrating in the upper atmosphere."

"Miles..." I repeated.

Just hearing her big brother's name filled me with the same kind of dread that the citizens of Heavenly Hill must have felt every time they read the morning headlines about a possible Russian attack.

Gwendolyn reached over and placed the palm of one hand on the moon's silver disk floating beside us. I waited for the apparition of a cosmonaut to take shape in the murky depths, grab her wrist, and pull her under. McKenna gave a panicked yap and sprang to his feet. He nudged her hand away with his snout and then jumped overboard. He was already out of arm's reach before either of us could stop him. After a long Midwestern winter and a fleeting spring, Lost Village Lake was still cold in early June, but this didn't discourage McKenna from paddling around the boat.

Gwendolyn slapped the hull.

"Stop being a naughty boy! Did you hear me? I swear I'll make you sleep in your crate tonight."

The dog ignored her empty threats and dove under the water.

"McKenna!" Gwendolyn cried. "McKenna!"

We looked on either side of the boat but saw no sign of him. I was about to invent an excuse for failing to dive in when, to my relief, McKenna resurfaced near the stern. I spun around on the bench, snagged his collar, and managed to haul him back on board.

Gwendolyn wrapped her arms around him. "You dumb dog! Why did you *do* that?"

McKenna pulled away from her and shook himself dry, drenching us both.

"That was a naughty thing to do," Gwendolyn scolded him. "No more boating for you."

Usually cowed by her anger, McKenna scratched behind his ear and retook his place at the bow, his tongue hanging happily from one corner of his mouth. He curled into a tight ball, and began to doze off as if nothing had happened.

Five

Only after tying up at the dock did I recall how, during our last week of class, Mr. Watts explained that the world had a funny way of playing tricks on us. Hands behind his back, hawkbill pipe clamped between his uneven teeth, he paced up and down the aisles.

"Sometimes," he said, "but especially in calm weather when it looks like a perfectly polished piece of glass, the lake effectively functions as a mirror and produces all sorts of interesting mirages. If a layer of cold air blankets the lake, topped by layers of increasingly warm air, the light bends, forming a lens. On some days, a house on the far side of the lake will look like it's just out of arm's reach. But on other days, the shoreline vanishes altogether. The human eye is also a kind of mirror. It takes in the world and reflects the world back. Unfortunately, there is too much visual information out there for our brains to process, at least the conscious part of our brains. Only the tiniest fraction of the human retina offers high-resolution vision."

Mr. Watts sat at the corner of his desk and gazed around the room at his students. He had a way of making it seem like he was speaking to each of us individually.

"For thousands of years, magicians, like the magicians of ancient Egypt who hardened Pharaoh's heart, have used this knowledge to their advantage when designing their enchantments. And to think modern science is only now catching up with these occult insights."

Maybe Mr. Watts was right. Maybe what I saw that night on Lost Village Lake was an optical illusion. Or maybe it was the result of pure exhaustion. I can only say the trip back to shore was slow going. Gwendolyn didn't say a word, and I could sense her disappointment in me. I tried to disguise my shame by rowing harder than before, but I seemed to be fighting a strong current. After fifteen minutes, I eased up on the oars and took a much-needed break. In the stillness of the night, I perceived a soft drumming. At first, I thought it was my heartbeat, but then I saw McKenna staring at me, his eyes locked on mine. Using his forepaws, he created a remarkably steady beat against Gwendolyn's bench.

"Some kind of trick?" I said, massaging my callused hands.

"No," she said, "but he keeps better time than the metronome on our piano."

McKenna stared harder at me and began drumming faster. I resumed rowing, trying to keep pace with the beat. Every time I eased up, he snorted and drummed with greater urgency, first the left paw, then the right. I chuckled at this but continued to row at the dog's preferred pace until the rhythm hypnotized me. I can think of no other explanation for what happened next.

As we glided along the water, the boat gradually faded away until it seemed to disappear beneath us. One moment, Gwendolyn and McKenna were sitting side by side at the bow; the next, they were levitating an inch above the water like a pair of yogis in deep meditation, their eyes closed, their bodies motionless. But rather than seeking peace of mind through the dissolution of the ego or petitioning a transcendent power, they seemed to be communicating with each other, hatching some elaborate scheme. The illusion lasted a few seconds before the boat reappeared and cut a path across the moonlit water.

At the dock, I struggled with the lines and clumsily tied up to the pylons. Making awkward excuses and stammering a hasty goodbye, I scrambled up the embankment, where I found my rusty wreck of a bicycle buried in the weeds. McKenna tried to follow me, but I yelled at him to stay. On a narrow trail that skirted the reservoir, I raced into the night.

Embarrassed by my cowardice, I forced myself to stop but didn't want to look back for fear I might glimpse a spinning silver disc rising from the lake bottom. Scanning the horizon for meteorites, I saw dense clusters of fireflies drifting over the reeds. Gwendolyn and McKenna stood by the skiff, their silhouettes outlined by the shimmering waves. I hurried away before they caught me staring, and pedaled through the dark toward the distant lights of town.

Six

Once it finally approved our application for the historical marker, a frustrating process that took nearly six months, the state permitted the committee to choose from three design options. The most popular was The Wakefield, but I argued that the plaque looked too much like a slate headstone in a forlorn cemetery ringed by a rusty wrought iron fence and creaking gothic gates. The second option was The Roadside, but with its rounded edges and antiquated font, this design looked too folksy to memorialize a girl who'd helped usher in the Space Age. After a heated discussion, the committee finally settled on The Funicular. It looked more modern than the others, maybe because the braided bronze rope bordering the plaque resembled a double helix, an encrypted code containing infinite creative potential, its origins and purpose wisely concealed from the eyes of man.

Of course, I see the world differently than most people. As a boy, I loved going to the new air-conditioned cinema on the square, where I sat through multiple screenings of *The Fly, Forbidden Planet, Invasion of the Body Snatchers,* and *The Day the Earth Stood Still.* A high-strung, accident-prone child who was never asked to play baseball in the park with the other boys, I spent an unhealthy amount of time speculating about future technologies and the dystopian world they were sure to usher in — ray-guns, truth serums, teleportation devices, cameras in the sky monitoring the movements of every citizen on planet Earth. At night, instead of studying for Mr. Watts' class, I read with philosophical fervor the science fiction pulp magazines then in vogue. With their harrowing tales of marooned astronauts on the rolling Martian dunes, secret meetings between interstellar bounty hunters in sinister spaceports, and renegade medical researchers hacking their way through impenetrable alien forests in search of psychoactive plants, these stories helped me make some sense of the otherwise inexplicable illusion I witnessed on the lake. The stories were more memorable than my ordinary life, and when something is memorable, it becomes a kind of truth, a truth more authentic than anything the adults in my life were open to believing.

While drafting the historical marker, I made an effort to think like a historian, that is to say, to think scientifically, to see everything in terms of cause and effect, but due to a strict word limit imposed on us by the state, the draft ran the risk of reducing Gwendolyn's life to a single event. I had to ask myself what information is essential to the passing traveler. Should I mention the mysterious object that plunged into Lost Village Lake and how it left an inedible mark on the wiry teenage boy who'd fallen helplessly in love with Gwendolyn Greene? Or should I describe how, a few weeks after that night on the lake, Gwendolyn received a letter from her brother Miles that would prove fateful.

To properly tell the story of Lieutenant Commander Miles Greene, we would need to commission another plaque. Known in town as the Handyman of the Heavens, Miles was a legendary Heavenly High quarterback, running up high scores on and off the field. Before graduating and joining the Air Force, he'd earned a reputation for being a fearless daredevil. During a friendly chicken race on County Road 216, he smashed up his old man's pickup truck and climbed unscathed from the twisted wreck, his teeth flashing white with movie-star perfection, his fierce Nordic blue eyes piercing through the smoke as if he'd just returned from the fens after slaughtering Grendel. Tall, broad-shouldered, tan even in winter, he seemed to be among life's Chosen Ones. During the final days of the Korean War, he flew several sorties deep into enemy territory and shot down a dozen enemy aircraft in single combat. Many years after the events described here, his luck would finally run out when, one stormy October night, he drowned at a blackjack table on a riverboat casino that collided with an iron ore tanker. The *Miss Bordereau* sank with five crew and ten passengers at the mouth of the Cuyahoga. Though he always made a point of being cruel to me, there is no question in my mind that the lieutenant died trying to save as many lives as he possibly could.

Until his untimely death, Miles served as a test pilot at the new NASA research center in Cleveland, and whenever he came home to visit, he always brought his little sister unusual gifts — a hunk of pink salt excavated from a mine fifteen hundred feet beneath Lake Erie; a fossilized trilobite excavated from the steep shale cliffs in the city's nature preserve; a typed draft of a scholarly paper, signed by Albert Michelson and Edward Morley, proposing an aether wind that carried light waves across the cosmos.

He often wrote Gwendolyn detailed letters. One was about a stray mutt he'd found roaming a park near headquarters. He and his colleagues adopted the dog as the agency's mascot and built a plywood shelter for him behind the jet propulsion lab. Named Ray in honor of Miles's favorite author, the dog had learned to endure conditions of extreme cold and hunger, and the engineers believed he would make the ideal specimen for an impending mission.

I don't need to tell you what we're up against, Gwendolyn. It's no secret that the Soviets intend to launch a dog into space. But if Ray successfully completes the training, we might have a real shot at beating the Russians and be the first country to send a living being into Earth's orbit. Children all over the world will read about Ray in history books. He'll be remembered as a national hero. Our boys in engineering will do everything in their power to bring Ray safely back home, but reentry is a tricky business and, if we're being honest, probably won't be perfected for years. For Ray, this will almost certainly be a one-way trip.

Like all Americans in those early days of space flight, Gwendolyn had seen plenty of newsreels with launchpads engulfed in flames and disintegrating rockets tumbling end over end into the ocean. She knew that, even if by some miracle the dog survived the launch, the poor thing would either freeze to death in the cold vacuum of outer space or burn up during reentry. Perhaps it was for the best when, twelve weeks before the launch, Ray became gravely ill with Lyme disease and had to be euthanized. There were other dogs in the training program, but none with so keen an intelligence, and now a last-minute search was underway to find a suitable replacement.

After reading this latest letter, Gwendolyn sent *The Sentinel*'s feature story about McKenna to Miles. Who knows why she was willing to put McKenna in such terrible danger? At first, she was thrilled by the idea of making history, but not even someone as clever as Gwendolyn could think through all the variables and anticipate so many unforeseen consequences.

Seven

In late June, on the morning before my fifteenth birthday, I heard an unusual rumble approaching Heavenly Hill. Terrified of another meteor bombardment, I sprang from my bed and looked out my window in time to see a long procession of military trucks and black sedans thundering down the street. At the square, the vehicles took a sharp left turn and disappeared over the hill. I knew exactly where they were going and why. I quickly dressed and, without saying goodbye to my mother, who insisted I eat breakfast, followed the dust trail that circled the edge of town.

I ascended a ridge and, from a quarter mile away, could see the new '57 Plymouth Fury belonging to Miles, its professionally polished bone-white finish reflecting the trucks lined up outside the Greenes' house. I coasted down the gentle slope and tossed my bike in the weeds beside the post and rail fence. A dozen unsmiling strangers wearing the cleaned and pressed uniforms of highly decorated military personnel stood under the shade of the Greenes' oak tree and observed McKenna weaving with lightning speed and agility through an obstacle course of orange cones and retractable nylon tubes. Another group of men in white shirt sleeves and black ties lowered their horn-rimmed glasses to check their stopwatches and jot notes on clipboards.

When he saw me, Miles strode with cowboy confidence across the backyard and fanned his face with his gray fedora.

"Hold up there, pudding," he said, raising a hand. "Can't you see grown men are conducting business? This is no place for children. We don't need a nosy schoolboy coming along and mucking things up."

"Just wanted to see what's going on," I said.

"Oh, you just wanted to see?" He flashed a mordant eye at me. "Well, son, the thing is, we're trying to minimize distractions and figure out if this dog has the right stuff. Now, you best hurry home to your comic books and chocolate bars."

"Where's Gwendolyn?"

Miles scratched his jaw, clean-shaven as always, and dabbed his forehead with a clean handkerchief. "Busy inside talking to important people. Why? You come here to put the moves on my little sister? Is that what you're up to, Romeo?"

"What? No! I'm not trying to put the moves on anyone."

Miles flicked the hat with his forefinger and thumb and watched it spin. "Must be something wrong with you then. You one of them funny boys? You like to hang out in the locker room? Ask your pals if they need help toweling off?"

"Huh?"

He stepped closer to me, his eyes changing color from ice-blue to hellfire red.

"Look," he said, brushing a bug from his arm and smoothing his sleeve, "I don't think Poochie Pie appreciates any interruptions. So, I'm going to count to three, okay?"

I smirked, arguably the most dangerous thing I've ever done in my life. I was seconds away from having my nose bloodied and my teeth knocked out. Lucky for me, McKenna abandoned the obstacle course and trotted over to greet me. He licked my hand and, with a series of snorts and sharp jerks of his head, asked me to follow him. Somehow, I understood what he was saying and jogged beside him down the embankment to the lake. Miles tried to stop me, but the military brass told him to stand down. A man operating a 16mm camera turned the lens in our direction and filmed us as we boarded the skiff.

Right away, McKenna sat at the bow and began drumming. I obediently tossed the lines on the dock, picked up the oars, and started to row. He set a steady tempo, and whenever he wanted me to change course, he let out a single sharp bark and jerked his head left or right. I like to think he was navigating by the unseen stars and that he had a precise destination in mind.

"Remarkable," the men said, scribbling furiously in their notebooks. "Extraordinary." One scientist even dared to utter the taboo word "miraculous."

For the next fifteen minutes, they observed us cruising back and forth along the lake while Miles, standing slack-jawed on the grassy slope, seemed to be devising some new cruelty for me.

Above the splash of waves, I could hear the sharp cry of gulls wheeling in the sky. I closed my eyes and for a moment felt like I was flying, my arms beating like wings in the warm summer air. When I opened them again, I saw Gwendolyn in a billowing blue summer dress standing at the back door, beaming with pride and waving to us.

Eight

Writers, generally speaking, tend to be a superstitious lot, and many of my fellow scribblers keep a memento mori at the corner of their desks. As for me, I keep an invitation in a plastic frame hanging on the wall of my one-room cabin. Despite self-exile to the sprawling Kingdom of Pauperdom, I try to keep the place up to code, so to speak. During arctic blizzards and interminable winter freezes, the big square-cut carpentry nails have an annoying habit of springing from the floors. I hammer them back into place, careful not to bruise the hardwood. I oil squeaking hinges, tighten dripping faucets, patch and sand small holes in the plaster, and adjust the wobbling blades of incorrectly calibrated ceiling fans. Once a week, I make sure to dust the framed invitation hanging above my bookcases. It chases away any hint of arrogance that may creep into my dark heart. From time to time, I glance at it, shocked by the grizzled reflection in the dusty glass. Postmarked September 10, 1957, the invitation itself is unremarkable — a small card on which is printed in bold black ink the time, date, and address of a dance hall in downtown Cleveland. Collectors have offered hundreds of dollars for it. I briefly entertained offers but could never bring myself to sell. You see, on the back of the card, scrawled in Gwendolyn's slanted hand, are two words in capital letters that possessed enough power to startle me out of my teenage stupor. To this day, they also remind me of my shameful weaknesses.

In the fall of 1957, when school was back in session, Gwendolyn was conspicuously absent. I hadn't seen her since that June morning on the lake, and for me, the summer quickly became a miserable gray blur. Three days after the military men visited her home, she and McKenna moved into the spare bedroom of her brother's brick bungalow in Cleveland. Each morning, at the new NASA research center and training facility, McKenna participated in rigorous training sessions with other dogs to determine if he could operate the controls inside a space capsule. Rudimentary computers were still too cumbersome for space flight, and those first primitive capsules required someone to work the controls manually. In the mornings, McKenna was taught to pull a series of small plastic levers and press a complicated pattern of blinking buttons. Once they were confident he'd memorized the correct sequence, the scientists and engineers recorded Gwendolyn's voice. They wanted to know if, rather than visual cues, McKenna could respond to verbal commands alone.

Finally, an official announcement was made. In November, McKenna would have the honor and distinction of piloting the Jupiter D spacecraft into lower Earth orbit, becoming the first living creature to leave our planet. NASA never made a secret of the mission — quite the contrary. Top brass believed the publicity would be good for the space program as well as national unity. Within hours, journalists from around the state descended on Miles's house, hoping to get a photograph of the lucky little dog.

In the weeks leading up to the launch, Gwendolyn and McKenna attained an astonishing level of celebrity. They were featured on magazine covers and appeared on dozens of news programs. Corporations used their likenesses on boxes of kibble and billboards advertising dog obedience training. In Heavenly Hill, everyone regarded Gwendolyn as a star, and as I sat in science class, barely listening to a visibly agitated Mr. Watts drone on about intelligent machines and something called a Turing Test, I wondered why we regarded certain people as "stars." Was it just the idolatry of the modern age? Or were some individuals truly touched in unique ways by mysterious cosmic forces?

One afternoon, having finished his training session at the space agency, McKenna and Gwendolyn were chauffeured downtown to a studio where they made their first live television appearance on a nationally syndicated variety show. The fast-talking host, enunciating each word through a mouthful of capped teeth, inquired about Gwendolyn's favorite song, her favorite subject in school, her favorite food, her favorite drink, her favorite color.

"And are you dating anyone special?" he wanted to know.

She hesitated before saying, "McKenna is the only boy in my life."

After a round of applause from the studio audience, the host asked, "Would your dog perform a few tricks for the folks watching at home? But first! Let's properly outfit our four-legged astronaut!"

From behind camera B, a stagehand appeared with a plastic prop that was supposed to be a space helmet but looked more like an empty fishbowl.

"What do you think, boy?" the host said. "Our talented staff in wardrobe designed this especially for you. Here, let me help you put this on."

McKenna backed away and growled.

Smiling apologetically at the cameras, Gwendolyn knelt beside him and whispered in his ear. McKenna nodded and gave three excited yaps.

"Is he ready, Gwendolyn? Yes? Okay, let's try this again!"

McKenna waited for the host to approach him, then snatched the microphone from his hand. He bolted to the opposite side of the stage and dropped the microphone near the curtain. Unamused by these antics, the host forced a toothy grin and walked over to retrieve the microphone.

"Charming," he muttered.

McKenna extended his front legs and crouched low to the ground.

"An absolute delight."

When the host bent over to pick up the mic, McKenna yanked the hairpiece from his head.

For the next five minutes, an eternity of broadcast time, McKenna had the audience in stitches. He shook the wig like a dead squirrel and tossed it high. There was a roar of laughter, hoots, and whistles as the hairpiece landed squarely on McKenna's head. He stood on his hind legs, the lopsided wig falling into his eyes, and danced back and forth across the stage. The 20-piece band struck up a brassy burlesque while the furious host, his hairless head gleaming under the unforgiving lights, tried to tackle him. McKenna was far too fast. He leaped atop the host's desk, lapped the coffee in his mug, and started chasing his tail. A blizzard of blue notecards flew across the floor while the bandleader waved his baton in a fascinating rhythm.

Gwendolyn stood in the wings and, until the producer asked her to put a stop to it, watched the spectacle with a satisfied smile.

Nine

A few days after this debacle, a famous Cleveland disc jockey, with the approval and full cooperation of space agency officials, announced a benefit concert for a local animal shelter. Organizers expected a huge turnout. On my hand-held transistor radio, the enthusiastic disc jockey shouted above a catchy jingle, "Make sure to bring your dancing shoes to the Moondog Coronation Ball, guys and gals, because it's gonna be a total *blast!*"

My personalized invitation arrived in the mail the following Saturday. Unfortunately, I had no way of getting to the dance. My mother, like so many respectable ladies in town, had never learned to drive, and I knew without having to ask that my father would flatly refuse to take me to the city. A man of high moral integrity who disapproved of girls inviting boys to social events, he grumbled incessantly about the price of gasoline and would have laughed at the suggestion he pay for us to stay overnight in a hotel, a luxury practically unheard of among the people of Heavenly Hill.

That night at the dinner table, I fidgeted helplessly with my fork and left my TV dinner untouched. In a despondent daze, I left the house and walked the streets of town. On the square, roused momentarily from my state of numb anxiety, I wandered into Book Your Trip and looked without much interest at the latest arrivals. Usually drawn to the science fiction paperbacks displayed on a table at the front of the store, I meandered to the section on philosophy, religion, and music. Borges, Bohm, Beethoven. A heavily annotated volume caught my eye. *Methuselah Variations: Musical Metamorphosis of Beethoven's Moonlight Sonata*. Rather than open the book to the table of contents or flip through the glossy back-and-white illustrations, I studied the title page with its elaborate copperplate engraving of a steely-eyed man with a mane of stormed-tossed, white hair. His cravat hung loosely around his upturned collar, and in his right hand, he held a dangerous-looking quill that might have doubled as a poisoned-tipped dart. The epigraph read, "Methuselah, they say, lived nine hundred years. But instead of years, maybe some composers live nine hundred lifetimes, each life a subtle variation on a single theme."

At that time, I had no interest in classical music and wasn't quite sure what I was trying to glean from the life of this temperamental, self-involved genius. I turned to the first chapter and read of young Ludwig's harrowing battle with smallpox; of his unsightly facial scars; of his lack of formal education; of his beloved mother Mary Magdalene, who at the age of forty, died of tuberculosis; of his tyrannical, alcoholic father who beat Ludwig without mercy and, for the most minor of infractions, locked him in the coal cellar. The catalog of horrors ran to hundreds of pages.

I returned the book to its place on the shelf and continued browsing. In the back of the store, a dozen men and women had formed a circle and sat listening to someone speak. I saw Mr. Lambert, Mr. Anderson, and even Mr. Greene. Then I heard a familiar British voice and recalled how Mr. Watts conducted bible study here on Saturday nights. I took a step back, pretending to peruse the other books.

"Saint Paul on pilgrimage. He's traveling to Naples to visit Virgil's tomb at the grotta vecchia. His back aches from carrying a leather satchel stuffed with dirty tunics. His worn sandals offer no arch support, and his calloused feet are starting to cramp. The sunny skies of southern Italy haven't been kind to his shaved head. He began losing his hair in his late teens, about the same time he had his first seizure, saw his first burst of blinding light, heard a chorus of reproachful voices, tumbled into a terrifying void. He asks himself again why he chose to journey on foot rather than sail from Rome. Financial problems. Legal fees. As a Roman citizen, he's entitled to his rights, but the upcoming trial before the emperor worries him. His correspondences with the palace have been lost to us, but we know from his surviving letters that Paul was a highly literate, thus formally educated, thus relatively affluent, thus exceptionally rare individual for his time and place. There are moments he regrets giving everything he owned to the poor."

Mr. Watts paused, and I could hear him pouring a drink. The proprietor, it seemed, was far more indulgent than the Episcopalian pastor who routinely condemned my teacher for his excesses. Other members of the bible study group shared his fondness for the bottle, and they did not object to the manner in which he scrutinized all of their facile assumptions and explored the funny ideas playing around the periphery of his imagination.

"A properly Hellenized intellectual from a prosperous merchant family, Paul was an early adopter — some have plausibly argued *inventor* — of a radical new philosophy. Levantine Buddhism. Even on pilgrimage, Paul advocates for spiritual peace through meditation and the renunciation of material possessions. The luxury beliefs of a spoiled young man? Before calling themselves Christians, the disciples tell anyone willing to listen that they are followers of the Way. To those sincerely seeking peace of mind, Paul says, 'Imitate the Way of Christ.' Never mind memorizing passages from scripture. The New Testament has yet to be written. The gospels, the pseudepigrapha, the gnostic texts, the psychedelic revelations on Patmos. As has been well-established by botanists, *psilocybe cubensis* grows in great abundance on the island's windward shore."

A profound silence enclosed the circle. Mr. Watts gazed deeply into his glass and then looked up, a flicker of curiosity in his eyes. I retreated behind a shelf, wondering if he'd spotted me.

"Committed to practicing the proven methods of a master, Paul travels on foot to Naples because Jesus demonstrated that walking was the correct Way to go on pilgrimage. 'Come, follow me.' The experience is an embodied one, not a metaphor, not an abstraction one reads in a self-help manual. Tradition tells us that when he finally arrived at the grotto, Paul fell to his knees and wept over Virgil's bones. Theologians speculate that had he but known him, Paul would have led Virgil to salvation. An intriguing possibility. Others find it strange that he wished to visit the grave of a pagan poet. Why not seek out a fellow traveler baptized in the Spirit? All of this comes from the voluminous annotations in my underscored edition of Dante's *Commedia*. But some mysteries can't be solved by reading a book."

Mr. Watts' voice sounded closer now, as if he'd left his seat and spoken to me from the other side of the shelf.

"Ah, but let me tell you how Virgil's shade spoke to Dante. 'Is your mind so distracted that you lose your pace? Why do you care what others are whispering? Just follow me and let people talk. Be like a sturdy tower that does not tremble in the fiercest wind. For any man who lets one thought — and then another — take him over will soon lose track of his goal.'"

I left the store, vaguely troubled by this story, and my thoughts soon returned to Gwendolyn. Indulging in heated adolescent fantasies, I envisioned slow dancing with her as a string orchestra played a lilting melody. I had it all carefully choreographed in my mind. When the clock chimed midnight, I would take her in my arms and, before kissing her, ask why on the back of the invitation she'd written in black magic marker, "HELP US!"

Ten

Every day after school, I went to the Heavenly Hill Library and spent an hour studying outdated road atlases, mapping out what I thought would be the best route to the city. I estimated that if I traveled at an average speed of ten miles an hour and allowed myself no more than two thirty-minute breaks, I could reach downtown Cleveland in under twelve hours. In the evenings, I worked in the garage, tuning up my bicycle, degreasing and oiling the chain, adjusting the seat and handlebars, checking the air pressure in my tires, and centering the brakes. I made a checklist of everything I intended to carry in my backpack — a change of clothes, two bottles of water, apples, and a bag of unshelled peanuts. As for the journey back home, I made no plans at all. Over the summer, I'd saved fifty dollars, more than enough for a motel room if I could find a proprietor willing to take a kid's money. If not, I'd happily sleep in an abandoned barn, a grain silo, or even an open field under the stars.

At dawn on an unusually warm Saturday morning in late September, I pedaled down my driveway and rode away from home. I couldn't decide if this journey was an act of rebellion against my parents or if it was a rescue mission. I had plenty of time to think about these matters as I traveled along backroads that stretched for mile after interminable mile. Field hands, accustomed to seeing tractors, combines, and the occasional Amish buggy, seemed mystified by the sight of a lone cyclist who waved but never slowed his pace.

Having traveled the better part of thirty miles, I encountered the first of many obstacles. An old covered bridge had collapsed into a ravine, and the detour added five miles to my journey. An hour later, as the unforgiving sun beat down on the treeless gravel road, I was set upon by a swarm of yellow jackets nesting in a fallen tree. Their stings were excruciating, and my calves burned for the rest of the day, but no matter how dejected I became, no matter how futile I believed my mission to be, I never once contemplated finding a payphone and calling my parents to rescue me. More likely than not, they hadn't even read the note I'd left on the kitchen counter and wouldn't notice my absence until suppertime. In those days, a child was expected to leave the house and not come home until the sun went down.

Fifty miles into my journey, I punctured my rear tire on a rusty nail at a railroad crossing. It took nearly thirty minutes to walk to the nearest gas station. From under a tin roof awning, the attendant flashed a silver-toothed grin. He sat on a folding chair, legs outstretched, hands behind his head. Despite the oppressive heat, he wore an olive-green field jacket, like the one I'd seen Miles wearing when he'd returned from Korea, with a name patch that said in black script *Stanley*.

"Can you fix a flat?" I asked, enviously eyeing the man's tiny sliver of shade.

He leaned over and spat a dark stream from the gap between his two front teeth.

"I pump gas and check under the hood."

He tipped his greasy cap in a courtly manner and smiled in a way that made me keep my distance.

"Well, can anyone give me a hand?" I implored.

"Mechanic be able to fix it for you."

"He's in the garage?"

"He didn't show up today. You want I should change the oil on that chain? Only cost you a dollar."

"A dollar? You're joking."

"Gotta charge you for material and labor."

I wiped the sweat from my eyes. "You have a soda machine?"

"Yep. But it ain't in working order. And it ain't been stocked in months. I sure could go for an ice-cold Coca-Cola right now, couldn't you?"

Stanley twisted his greasy cap, stuck a long-nailed finger in his mouth, and dug around his left cheek until he dislodged an impressive plug of tobacco. Before tossing it to the ground, he felt compelled to sniff it.

"Well, can I at least refill my water bottle?" I asked.

"Nope."

"But you must have a hose."

"That I do, young fella. That I do."

"Then why can't I use it?"

"On account of the owner didn't pay the water bill. Didn't pay his employees either. That's how come the mechanic ain't here today. Times is tough, case you couldn't tell. I'm here only because I have nothing better to do."

"How about tools? Can I borrow an adjustable wrench?"

"Sure, got plenty of wrenches. Adjustable wrenches, socket wrenches, even a crazy-looking dog bone wrench. But I gotta charge you a fee. You'll be wanting a patch and some glue, I expect."

I tried reasoning with him, pleaded poverty, but he refused to budge on the price. In the end, I reluctantly handed over a five-dollar bill. Stanley lugged a toolbox from the garage.

"Let's see now…"

He handed me a greasy wrench, a rubber patch, and a crusty tube of adhesive. Then he took his seat in the shade and watched me through the shimmering solar haze.

I knelt beside the pumps streaked with iron-red dust. Stunted weeds flowered among the cracks in the pavement, their pale colors blanched by the sunlight. I fumbled with the back wheel, my eyes stinging with sweat, and managed to catch my hand on the spinning crank.

Stanley whistled. "Close one, son. For a second there, I thought you lost your pinkie. Not that you need it. Better watch those thumbs, though. Hard to get along in this world without thumbs. Saw men like that in Shanghai. Coolies used fishing knives on themselves to get out of the service."

After patching the inner tube and inflating the tire, I tossed the wrench to the ground and pedaled away. Stanley rose from his chair and turned his eyes to me. First, he made a show of putting the cash in his shirt pocket and patting his chest, then he stood at attention, raised his right hand, and saluted me. For the next hour, I could think of nothing except that odd little man with thinning hair and half-crazed grin.

Eleven

Later that afternoon, indifferent now to boredom and dehydration, I passed through the ruins of an abandoned mill town, its crooked streets littered with shattered glass. From there, I pedaled under a tunnel of hemlock trees, their limbs creaking against the wind, their shadows casting alien shapes on the road. Grateful to have escaped momentarily from the burning sun, I rested there for a few minutes before continuing on my journey.

For the rest of the day, I wobbled along one desolate stretch of road after another. I was beginning to lose hope that I would ever reach my destination, but at dusk, I saw a hopeful sign. Rising from the brambles and tall grass, a flying saucer flashed its lights three times. The spacecraft hurtled toward me at an alarming rate of speed, but somehow, I knew it had come in peace. While I waited for its trajectory beam to lift me into the sky and whisk me away to a refreshing waterfall or a cool mountain stream, I watched the UFO transform into a rattling pickup truck, its front fender tied up to the rusted frame with kite string.

"Hop in," a voice commanded.

I vaguely recall looking at the bearded face of a young man glowing green in the dashboard light. I was so dazed by then I couldn't be entirely sure if I was speaking to a man or a creature glimpsed in the reptile enclosure of a roadside zoo.

"What planet are you from?" I muttered.

My driver laughed and lowered the volume on the radio. "I know, I know. You country boys don't dig jazz, do you?"

Together, we traveled for many miles, my bike jostling against the truck bed. I wanted nothing more than to fall asleep in the cab, but my driver wouldn't stop talking music — chord progressions, key changes, harmonies — until we reached the city's outskirts. A student at a Jesuit university in Cleveland, his dream was to make a small contribution to the music industry.

"Open a record store. Manage a club and promote interesting new acts. Or maybe start an independent record label. My parents disapprove, of course. They call me their imp, a nickname they gave to their little noisemaker. I learned to play records on their stereo before I was three years old. That's what they tell me anyway. Lots of Mitch Miller. They had a few jazz albums. Fitzgerald, Satchmo, Sinatra. Otherwise, they're pretty square. They don't go for any hip stuff. Charles Mingus. John Coltrane. They don't dig it. That's how I am about rock and roll. Don't be fooled, my friend. Rock is a fad. If folk music and ballads from the old country are the language of the past, jazz is the language of the future. Ever been to Los Angeles? Last time I was there, I heard this young band leader. Just released an album called *The John Towner Touch*. Not much older than me and already losing his hair. Seemed to be falling out as he pounded away at the piano. Word is he's destined to become the next Bernard Herrmann. Spacey, you know. Far out. But not like the racket I heard in Hamburg. Went to a club to hear these Scousers calling themselves the Quarrymen. Looked like punks up there, experimenting with electric guitars and wah-wah pedals. They'll find out soon enough that technology has its limits."

He laughed and glanced at the guitar case on the floor. Like me, my driver packed light.

"Listen to me. Who am I to talk, right? I'm no artist. Oh, I can play chords, pick out a melody, but I have no natural ability. No gifts." His smile faded a little. "The wise men didn't follow my star and come bearing gifts. I wonder which star they did follow. Sirius? Alpha Centauri? Or did they look for a comet? A supernova?"

At some point, I'm not sure when, the landscape gradually changed. The farms became public parks, and the roads became winding boulevards lined with regal Tudor houses. With their decorative poplars and persimmons set against immaculately maintained lawns and lush flowerbeds, every property resembled an ornate botanical garden straight out of a glossy magazine. When we reached campus, my driver insisted on taking me to the dining hall to buy me a Coca-Cola and a chocolate bar. He drew a map and scribbled directions on a notepad. Then, while walking me back outside, he suddenly stopped and scowled.

"This space race with the Russkis is making people bonkers, don't you think? Rockets, missiles, hydrogen bombs. And now they're putting on some big show before blasting a dog into outer space. What sort of lunatic civilization would do such a dastardly thing?"

He shook his head and ripped from a bulletin board a rainbow gradient poster urging students to purchase tickets for tonight's Moondog Coronation Ball.

Twelve

My first experience in the big city was a harrowing one.

To the wail of sirens and the sound of a distant train, I rode down a hill into a smoking hellscape of blast furnaces, slag heaps, and mountains of luminous ash, their peaks rising above the steel mills like the painted cones of volcanoes. Despondent men in hardhats stood like prisoners behind barbed-wire fences, watching blue smoke swirl from smokestacks hundreds of feet tall. Next, I pedaled by a brick warehouse the size of a city block, a relic from the sweatshop days before the enactment of child labor laws when kids as young as eight and nine were sent by their half-starving parents to work twelve-hour shifts at the looms and presses, miserable little boys and girls, their faces sparkling with graphite dust, their tiny fingers darting between the spindles of those unforgiving high-speed machines. If Gwendolyn had been around in those days, she would have been a professional saboteur. Within an hour of entering the building, she would have cut every wire, jammed every gear, and snapped every lever. An entire army of cigar-chomping overseers, their eyes scanning the floor for whimpering slackers, would have been hard-pressed to catch her in the act.

On a heavily trafficked street where, for no apparent reason, the drivers blared their horns, I saw men stumble cursing from mean, windowless taverns and stagger along curbs piled high with uncollected trash. From a tangle of sagging powerlines, an invisible bird cawed mockingly at them. On an avenue lined with the scattered shells of rusted cars, I passed an abandoned church, its chipped and broken masonry covered in graffiti. In the crooked streets, dogs squatted indifferently, and loud laughter erupted from open windows. Under the buzzing streetlights, a fine sodium tinged ash-coated rooftops and doorways.

Outside a sprawling apartment complex, a woman at a crosswalk brandished her cane and told me to look where the hell I was going. In an alleyway, I eyed a group of tough-looking teenagers pitching pennies. They observed me as they might a rat scuttling from a sewer. One of them waved me over and invited me to play, but I kept moving.

Weaving between streetcars and busses, I finally reached downtown. On an avenue awash in neon lights, throngs of people rushed along sidewalks and streamed from the revolving doors of department stores. I tried and failed to imagine Gwendolyn living in a place like this. Everything was either fixed in stone or frozen in glass and steel. Here and there, I saw a tree or a small patch of grass, but anything that hinted at nature felt artificially arranged, like bad stagecraft. By surrounding themselves with the illusion of permanence, the citizens of this sprawling, industrial metropolis had confused the eternal with ugly buildings and statues of corrupt politicians. Nature was never fixed. It was in constant motion. It danced. It wiggled. Only after my adventure had ended did it occur to me that the Moondog Coronation Ball was also a simulacrum of nature, a hastily conceived ritual intended to mimic our natural yearning for the ecstatic, the transcendent, the beautiful.

At a busy corner, a street vendor lifted a metal lid and released a dizzying cloud of boiled hotdogs. Weak-kneed from the savory smoke wafting from the stalls, I stopped outside the dance hall and dismounted my bike. A man reeking of gin grabbed my arm and sputtered something about the mannequins in the storefront windows.

"Robots!" he said. "Look at them. Computers with superhuman intelligence. They're recording our every move. Biding their time until they can conquer the planet. I'll sing for them now. I'll sing for them! Tra-la-la!"

Without thinking to lock my bicycle, I gripped my backpack and nearly tripped as I sprinted up the steps. I hadn't arrived until the event was well underway, and when I pushed open the heavy double doors, I found myself in a smoke-filled lobby crammed with hundreds of people. Drenched in sweat, my face filthy with road dust, I searched for a restroom to change into a fresh shirt and wash the grit from my eyes.

An usher blocked my path. "Ticket."

"I'm a guest," I rasped.

He looked me up and down, his lips curling into a sneer. "A guest?"

"Yes, Gwendolyn Greene invited me."

The usher's bland, gray eyes regarded me with amusement. "Good one, kid. Show is sold out, okay? Need a ticket to get in."

I searched my backpack for the invitation. "Just a second."

"Gotta be eighteen or older, too. You eighteen?"

"No, but you see —"

"Can't admit you if you're not eighteen."

I could see he was hoping for an excuse to drag me outside and, for good measure, shove me down the stairs like a theater critic punishing the author and principal star of an unhappy farce.

On stage, three guitarists howled into their microphones. The drummer hit the snare every other beat, measure after measure, a relentless driving rhythm that felt like someone drilling holes into my head. Men in dark suits and sunglasses, paying no attention to what was happening onstage, patrolled the floor and studied every face in the crowd. After the final crashing chord, a man in a bowtie and bespoke plaid suit jogged across the stage and winked at a camera in one of the boxes. It was only then that I realized there were cameras everywhere.

"Let's hear it," said the MC, "for Isaac and the Space Kidettes! Wonderful! And now, ladies and gentlemen, if I can please have your attention, it's the moment you've all been waiting for!"

The lights dimmed. The crowd grew quiet. In his hand, the MC held a small crown he raised for all to see.

"That's right, it's time to ordain the Hound of the Heavens, the Canine of the Cosmos, the Mongrel of the Milky Way, not to mention the most perceptive pooch on our planet. My friends, I give you the new Sovereign of the Starry Skies, everyone's favorite four-legged friend, McKenna!"

In three enormous leaps, McKenna came bounding from the wings and sat at the MC's feet. A moment later, Gwendolyn walked on stage and waved to the crowd. Instead of the saddle shoes, paisley blouse, and Capri jeans she wore during previous public appearances, Gwendolyn now wore white Mary Janes and a sea foam green dress, its tulle embroidered with sequined flowers and layered-over taffeta. Under all of those lights, she looked startled to find herself in such a frightening carnival of a place, a dazzling fairy blown from the pages of a forgotten childhood storybook.

With feigned reverence, the MC took a knee and placed the crown on McKenna's head. While the audience whooped and cheered, reporters snapped a hundred pictures. They shouted at Gwendolyn to turn this way, turn that way. Lower your eyes, raise your chin. Smile. The band started up again. This time, the quartet bobbed their heads and shrieked about bikini-clad Martian girls. McKenna seemed to thrive on the energy in the hall. The crown fixed firmly on his head, he trotted with ease along a balance beam, jumped through three fiery hoops, and raced back and forth on a teeter-totter.

It dawned on me that this almost certainly would be the last time I'd ever see McKenna. He and Gwendolyn were scheduled to board a military plane to make final preparations for November's rocket launch at Cape Canaveral. Desperately shouting his name, I yanked my arm from the doorman and darted between the happy couples dancing in the hall. I was tossed around a turbulent sea of bodies and found myself flailing toward the stage. People pressed in close. Elbows jabbed my ribs. Women stepped on my feet, their sharp heels grinding into my toes. I frantically waved my arms above my head, trying any way I could to signal McKenna, but everyone wanted to get a glimpse of the world's first space traveler and shoved me toward an emergency exit. In the confusion of cameras and flashing bulbs, I lost sight of Gwendolyn as she disappeared in the wings.

The only way to reach McKenna was by levitating above the floor the way he had levitated above the lake. All I needed to do was concentrate and contact him using my mind. From the back of the hall, I saw his silhouette glide across the stage. I breathed more deliberately, counting the intervals between each inhalation and exhalation.

"Focus," I whispered.

My eyes fixed on McKenna with hypnotic intensity, and soon my panic subsided. McKenna stopped dashing around and sat center stage. He gazed over the auditorium as if searching for me and began drumming with his paws. Suddenly, the room became cooler, my body lighter, the music much sweeter than before, a rhapsodic doo-wop with rich harmonies. Pale light filtered through stained-glass windows and fell in thin green pools on the dance floor.

The hall slowly turned into a crystal-clear lake. All I had to do now was swim through its rejuvenating waters. I closed my eyes and, losing my precarious claims to reality, became one with McKenna's confident, guiding beat. First, my heels, then my toes lifted an inch from the floor. Unable to believe how simple it was, this aquatic ballet, I raised my arms and began doggy paddling. Then, a gentle hand fell on my shoulder and pulled me back to Earth. Above the distant hum of the crowd, I heard a familiar voice.

"I *knew* you'd come."

I jumped as if startled from a dream and, expecting to see the angry doorman, found myself staring into Gwendolyn's eyes.

She pressed her face against my shoulder and hugged me with both arms.

"Why are you crying?" I asked.

"I've made a terrible mistake," she said.

"A mistake?"

"I don't want them to take McKenna. I don't want them to take my dog."

"You don't?"

"I want to go home. I want to go home right now."

"Did you tell them? The engineers? The scientists?"

"They say it's too late now. Please, you must help me save McKenna." She was sobbing so hard that she could barely speak the words. "You *must* help us. You *must*."

"Don't worry, Gwendolyn, I'll help you."

But the truth was I didn't know how to help her, and I didn't know how to respond when I heard another voice say, "My God, kid, what the hell *happened* to you?"

Gwendolyn gasped and stumbled away from me.

Through an expanding contrail of cigarette smoke, Lt. Commander Miles Greene parted the crowd by raising his hands and marched over to us. The heavy musculature of his face seemed to relax, and he repeated the question with what sounded like genuine concern. Yes, what the hell *did* happen to me? I found the question an interesting one and tried to think of a reasonable answer. But by then, the room had started to spin in a furious kaleidoscope of color. My knees buckled, and I collapsed to the floor.

Thirteen

According to the historical marker, at dawn on November 27, 1957, three Air Force officers put McKenna in a harness and led him to a launchpad at Cape Canaveral. Outfitted for the mission in a special spacesuit, McKenna was by all accounts well-tempered and seemed eager to ride the elevator three-hundred-sixty feet to the capsule atop the rocket. The compartment was so small that only one man could squeeze inside to strap McKenna to the padded box designed to stabilize his body. Before securing the hatch, the three men stood shoulder to shoulder on the platform and saluted him.

The launch site was strictly off-limits to civilians. Spectators, including Gwendolyn, who'd been denied access to the mission control center, had to watch from the beach just south of the launch site. The generals didn't want to deal with an emotionally distraught teenage girl should anything go awry. Newspaper and television reporters formed a continuous palisade along the shore. Like pilgrims who'd traveled enormous distances to witness a miracle, they spoke in appropriately reverential tones and predicted that in a decade or two, the average American would be vacationing in space hotels orbiting the Earth. By the end of the century, they said, there would be colonies on the moon and military bases on Mars. They speculated about the possibility of human clones, telecommunications satellites, and artificial intelligence. Now, they waited for the revivifying power of modern technology to work its magic.

At precisely 11:27 AM, with a gentle ocean breeze blowing across the cape, the Jupiter's five engines rumbled to life in a slow, grinding pulse. Up and down the beach and fishing pier, people cheered as the engines grew louder and louder. On the beach, a little boy, standing with his toes in the water, released a dozen bright balloons when the rocket ignited and lifted from the launchpad. The entire beach swayed and surged. Onlookers raised their hands to shield their eyes from the glare. Brilliant sunlight flickered off their portable radio sets and diamanté glasses. Sluggish waves broke at their feet.

At least, that's how I imagined the scene. I wasn't there. After my misadventures on the road, I was no longer permitted to leave the house. Like everyone else in Heavenly Hill, I watched the gray plume on a fuzzy black and white television screen, so I can't say if Gwendolyn gasped when the first stage rocket, rather than gain momentum and arc smoothly above the Atlantic, began to wobble ominously back and forth. I don't know if she screamed when the rocket started to burn out of control or if she fell to her knees when orange flames shot from the booster. And I certainly cannot describe her anguish as she watched the disintegrating debris plummet from the distant offshore haze and plunge piece by fiery piece into the huge swells. Had I been with Gwendolyn in Florida, I would be unable to describe the pain she experienced. After all, how does one describe the indescribable?

I expect Miles was at her side, but he may have been in the control room trying to determine if a terrified McKenna, sealed within the pressurized capsule, had panicked and pulled the wrong lever. I only know that the rocket, having accelerated to one thousand miles per hour, collapsed in midair and disappeared in a blinding pillar of light. A team of NASA engineers, practiced in the fine art of obfuscation, would later attribute the catastrophe to "an evaporation of fuel and a short circuit."

A thin autumn rain fell on our drab little town that day, and a light mist hung among the trees. I stood in my living room, staring at the TV screen. My parents turned to me with empty expressions. They didn't say anything. Probably, they were afraid to speak. I shot them an accusatory glare and bolted out the door. I ran down the street and continued running until I reached Lost Village Lake. For the rest of the day, I walked the lake's perimeter, the impossibly distant sun veiled by a cold mist, my inconsolable cries hanging in the damp autumn air.

Mr. Watts always said the lake was a place of enchantment, of miraculous cures, of startling changes in destiny, but as I watched the raindrops striking the water, it seemed the summer magic had faded forever, and all that remained was a lusterless gray sheen that reflected the world's grim realities.

Fourteen

Back home that night, drifting off into a restless slumber, I thought I heard McKenna's whimpers as he clawed at the walls of the burning capsule. He seemed to be crying out to me and Gwendolyn, asking why we'd done this to him. Was he being punished for being a bad boy? Had he done something wrong? He begged us to make it stop. With a scream lodged in my throat, I sat up in bed, drenched in sweat. For a long time, I listened to the cold November air lance around the loose window casements.

Desperate to drown out these wretched sounds, I jumped from my bed and paced the room. Still recovering from the dream, I went to my desk and flipped through the spiral notebook I used in science class. I'd never felt inclined to write anything in my life, even when compelled to do so by Mr. Watts, who was always asking for book reports on Charles Darwin and Alan Turing, but now, squinting at my indecipherable notes on thermodynamics, gravity, and mechanics, I chewed on an already badly masticated pencil and began to fill page after page until my wrist ached and my pencil was reduced to a useless yellow nub.

To call the clumsily worded jumble of ideas a short story would be inaccurate. Unlike the science fiction stories I read in the pulps, my late-night scribbles struck me as murky, indistinct, difficult to categorize. The sentences felt dreamy, slightly out of control, more like a fable or a prophecy, but instead of tearing the pages from the notebook and tossing them in the trashcan, I began to revise what I'd written.

The next morning, ignoring the sympathetic stares from neighbors, I went to the library and typed the story from my notes, correcting errors and expanding on my initial ideas. The work became a refuge for me, a world formed entirely from the materials of my mind, and I found that I preferred the secure realities of my imagination to the endlessly bizarre fictions of everyday life.

For weeks, I hesitated, but on a blustery winter night, under a sky shimmering with stars, I walked with envelope in hand to the post office and mailed the manuscript to *T-Minus One: A Magazine of Speculative Fiction.* The editor must have guessed right away that the story was the work of a mere child and rank amateur, but rather than discard my manuscript with the other unremarkable submissions drawn from the slush pile, he had the kindness to send me a handwritten note. He pointed out the story's merits and encouraged me to continue to develop my craft. With that, the first of many rejection letters, I knew I had found my one true calling. Books. Pen and paper. A commitment to the dark art of storytelling. Dark because a story always conceals something important, even from its creator.

Gwendolyn, on the other hand, had trouble finding solace after the tragedy. She politely declined an invitation from Mr. Watts to address the student body in the high school auditorium. She even refused to attend the ice cream social and candlelight vigil held on the town square to honor the memory of her heroic dog.

To my astonishment, Gwendolyn returned home to Heavenly Hill for just a day, long enough to collect her belongings and say her goodbyes. I never really pictured her as a social climber, but her brush with fame had opened many doors. Before the launch, she'd already decided to attend a prestigious all-girls academy on a full scholarship, the sort of place where students dressed in plaid skirts and navy blazers and took riding lessons in the afternoons.

"I'll never fit in at some fancy boarding school," she said, "but I also know I can't stay here. Not anymore. Too many ghosts."

We stood beside a snowdrift in her front yard, both of us finding it hard to look the other in the eye. Miles, loading her things in the trunk of his Fury, took a break and walked over to shake my hand. After the Moondog Coronation Ball, he'd bought me a meal at an all-night diner and then drove me back to Heavenly Hill. My bicycle was long gone, stolen perhaps by that strange man singing to the mannequins in the storefront windows. My parents assured me that my traveling days were over, but now, as we said our goodbyes, Miles presented me with a new baby blue Schwinn.

"Carry on, soldier," he said, stood at attention and saluted me.

Gwendolyn kissed me on the cheek.

Mr. Greene and I watched her drive away with Miles. We kept waving until the Fury disappeared over the snowfields and distant hills. Mr. Greene turned away without speaking, and I could see the tears in his eyes. Although the world made less and less sense to him, he understood a father's responsibility to his daughter and probably believed he'd failed her in some crucial way. For my part, I believed I'd failed her as a friend. We had this one thing in common, and until I left Heavenly Hill a few years later, it became our unspoken bond.

Fifteen

A week after the launch, Mr. Greene had hundreds of feet of lumber delivered and neatly stacked behind his house. Curious neighbors drove by and saw him wandering among the wooden pyramids like some rural pharaoh, contemplating the prospect of his embalmment. He made no mystery of his intentions. Years ago, he'd promised his daughter a treehouse, and now he was making good on that promise. But to what end, now that Gwendolyn had left home? I suspect he was looking for a way to occupy his mind and keep the demons at bay.

Although he had no formal training as a carpenter, he'd developed a talent for woodcarving and was proficient with a hammer and nails. Notoriously tight with a dollar, he splurged on a circular saw, a smoothing plane, a sander, and a power drill. In the pocket of his flannel shirt, he kept a notepad and pencil, and on a leather belt hanging from his hips, he carried a trusty tape measure. Seldom taking time to eat a proper meal, scurrying like a squirrel through the warren of makeshift compartments, Mr. Greene labored day and night in his backyard so that, when the seasons came wheeling back around to spring, the treehouse was beginning to take shape.

One night, while riding my new Schwinn past his house, I saw a blaze of candlelight through the budding branches. Encased in an exoskeleton of plywood and 2x4s, the white oak looked like a dystopian high-rise, not unlike the ones I saw in Cleveland. At some point that spring, he took up residence in its bird-infested rooms and rarely entered his home. To bathe, he used a garden hose and stood naked under the icy spray of water like a penitent making amends for his sins; to listen to the ballgames on the radio, he ran an orange electric cord from the house to the tree; and to prepare his meals, he made do with the coal-burning grill on his patio. Warding away the robins and sparrows proved difficult. On the window ledges, he placed plastic owls and rubber snakes.

In May, he constructed a conical spire atop the highest floor. People complained they could see it from miles away and said it looked like a demented countryside chapel. Only then did the town's council decide the time had come to take action. In those days, Heavenly Hill had strict codes against the construction of tall structures. During their monthly meeting, council members drafted a new amendment to the charter, retroactively including treehouses as part of this sanction. The measure passed with only one dissenting vote. Before adjourning the meeting, Mr. Watts, the council president, volunteered to break the news to Mr. Greene since no one else was willing to do it. When they returned to their homes that night, the members found taped to their front doors handwritten invitations, cordially inviting them to attend a Memorial Day barbecue in Mr. Greene's backyard.

Half the town was in attendance that sunny afternoon. One hundred or so guests mingled in the backyard by the lake, and Mr. Greene, who'd draped his treehouse in festive twinkle lights, encouraged everyone to take self-guided tours through the funhouse confusion of rooms. Those of us who could manage it eagerly climbed the ladder and entered through the tight, splintered hole at the bottom.

Though the work of an obvious apprentice, Mr. Greene's carpentry proved structurally sound and surprisingly resilient to the forces of nature. Painted in vibrant colors — periwinkle, persimmon, pomegranate — the interiors served practical functions. On the lower level, for example, we found a laundry room with a galvanized steel tub and retractable clothesline, a storage room stocked with canned goods and mason jars, and a kitchenette complete with a varnished board and old crate that served as table and chair. Higher up, Mr. Greene had constructed a game room with shelves on which he'd reverentially placed

Gwendolyn's childhood dolls and favorite board games. There was even a small library ("an athenaeum," he called it) with her magazines and paperbacks. In one of the upper-level rooms, where there was a break in the canopy, he'd built an observatory decorated with sky charts and science fiction movie posters. *The Blob, The Thing, Attack of the 50 Foot Woman*. We found a sleeping bag on the floor and, next to the window, a telescope mounted on a tripod.

Everyone else, too old or tired to continue the steep ascent, stayed behind, but I kept climbing the ladders higher and higher until I reached the uppermost room with its strange conical spire twisting through the canopy. I probably gasped when my eyes finally adjusted to the flickering light of votive candles and saw how Mr. Greene had carved into the tree trunk the faces of his wife, son, and daughter. He'd even carved a likeness of McKenna.

Luckily, no one was inside the treehouse when the fire started later that night.

I'd already left the party with my teetotaling parents, but from what I heard over the next few days, the remaining guests were getting pretty rowdy. Mr. Greene, commandeering the grill dangerously close to the tree, squirted lighter fluid on the glowing coals. Mr. Watts tried to warn him, but Mr. Greene laughed quietly to himself and shook his head. Under his breath, he uttered a curse or incantation and then sprayed more fluid on the grill. He stumbled from the violent whoosh of flames but didn't attempt to douse the fire, not that the garden hose would have done him much good. Even when the popping embers floated through the open windows and ignited the wood planks like cheap kindling, Mr. Greene seemed more concerned about the blackened brats and burgers than the treehouse.

The fire spread so quickly that he and his guests had to seek refuge on the dock, the great placid back of the lake turning crimson in the firelight. Fifteen minutes later, the town's sole fire engine arrived, but by then, the fire was burning with such intensity that the exploding limbs echoed like gunshots and then came crashing to the ground.

By dawn, the limbless oak looked like a smoldering black monolith. Those who stayed until morning laughed at Willard Anderson, who'd fallen asleep in the rowboat, an empty bourbon bottle tucked under his arm. The guests spoke of insurance policies, loss of property, and possible criminal charges. They talked about anything at all so long as they made no mention of their complicity in Mr. Greene's nervous breakdown, they who understood his anguish but lacked the fortitude to intervene and offer their support.

For the next year, Mr. Greene worked the farm, but eventually, he sold the land, the alpacas, and all his equipment. The move to town was a difficult transition for him, and he never entirely acclimated himself to it, a man used to wide open spaces and starry skies. He often lamented the light pollution in town. During my senior year, I would see him sitting alone at the bookshop, drinking coffee and staring blankly at the passersby. Sometimes, I would stop in to peruse the magazines and say hello. Neither of us mentioned the treehouse or his cherished white oak, and we never brought up the subject of Gwendolyn or McKenna.

Today, all that remains of the tree is a blackened stump. Unaware of its significance, most visitors don't even notice it. Why would they? For me, it has become a sacred sight, a place for reflection on the past and possible future. Even now, while sitting at my writing desk, I can sometimes hear Mr. Greene's distant hammering, and I can still see the four tempered faces buried beneath a thin layer of charcoal and ash.

Sixteen

Much to my parents' chagrin and increasing concern, I became more withdrawn after graduating high school and kept mainly to myself. Even then, I dreamed of becoming a published author, but the pulps were going out of business, and financial opportunities, even modest ones, for an aspiring young writer were few and far between. Still, I persevered, as a true believer must, and in time, managed to place my stories in obscure literary journals. It occurred to me, almost with the power of revelation, that I must reject the usual middle-class script — college, career, marriage, children, an acrimonious divorce after many years of mutual anguish — and instead dedicate my life to a higher calling. Not God precisely. No, nothing so conjectural.

At eighteen, with no money and no prospects for steady employment, I left home and hitchhiked across the country. I thought writers were supposed to do things like that: working odd jobs, making poor choices professionally and romantically, drinking too much, struggling to make ends meet. I lived at various times at the edge of western deserts and on storm-battered barrier islands. I slept in tents and under bridges and shared apartments with drifters that I thought might try to rob and kill me while I slept.

During these years, Gwendolyn and I exchanged the occasional letter, but as time passed, her letters arrived with less regularity. Most were brief, sometimes no more than a few sentences scribbled on the back of a postcard. From what she told me, it sounded like she was leading a charmed life, traveling to faraway cities, seeing the world, and meeting fascinating people. I was happy for her and wished her well.

Eventually, her letters stopped coming altogether.

After twenty-five years on the road, I received news that my father was seriously ill, and I returned home to Heavenly Hill.

Except for the small obituary in *The Sentinel*, there was no notice about his sudden passing a few weeks later. I didn't think to contact Gwendolyn, not that I'd even know how to get in touch anymore since Mr. Greene had passed away years ago. While sorting through my dad's personal effects in the basement, I stumbled upon a box of my discarded manuscripts, including that first short story I'd written in high school. When I read it again, I rediscovered the joy of storytelling and felt like I was fourteen years old again. There seemed to be a hidden intelligence within its pages, and I spent the next year expanding it into my first novel. In one sense, my story had nothing at all to do with Gwendolyn, but in another sense, it had everything to do with her, and it proved to be a catalyst for our final meeting.

Set in the near future and drawing on a number of significant details from my own experience, *IMPETUS 13 and the Constitutional Crisis of 2057* concerns a world in which work is obsolete, physical labor shunned, marriage outlawed. For companionship, citizens have government-issued IMPs that float freely beside them wherever they go. The IMPs emit low bleating sounds, like baby alpacas, and rotate counterclockwise as they hover through hallways and glide down streets. Unlike previous cylindrical models, the new and improved IMP 13.0 is spherical, completely translucent, and feels soft to the touch, a gelatinous mass of pulsating blue-green electrodes. Some people complain that the updated IMP looks too much like a human brain, its ever-expanding tendrils forming a web of complex circuitry. Others say it looks like an unblinking eye. Still others believe it looks like a miniature planet that, in its predictable orbit around its owner, changes from cloudy blue to a deep mossy green.

In a fully automated society, these orbs take care of basic human needs, communicating with lower-order machines to prepare meals, wash dishes, fold laundry, and administer medication to a society that has become irretrievably dependent on powerful pharmaceuticals. Faced with an epidemic of boredom and spiraling depression, humanity has come to an existential crossroads. Revolution is in the air. What people really crave is trouble. Lots of trouble. They yearn for uncertainty, anxiety, failure, death. They want to fall in love and start families. Activists demand an amendment to the Constitution, prohibiting machines from doing what human beings are capable of doing for themselves. Without a sense of adventure, they argue, life loses its value and meaning. People need a daring mission, knowing they may fail. There is, of course, a critical caveat to this legislation — citizens must be prepared to endure the consequences of their actions, so it's best to behave in a manner that suggests the consequences are worth it.

Published by a small press in 1984 under the fanciful pseudonym D.P. Mere, my novel failed to garner much attention from reviewers, and with its limited print run, I lamented that no one would ever read it for the simple reason that no one would know of its existence. But within a week of the novel hitting the shelves, I received an unexpected letter from Gwendolyn Greene, inviting me to her home to sign her copy.

> *Some old acquaintances told me about your book, so I rushed out and bought a dozen to give to friends and family. I loved every page! And I thought it clever how you alluded to Heavenly Hill. But why on earth did you use an alias?*

I happily agreed to the meeting but never told her why I'd chosen a pen name. To be honest, I hadn't given the matter much thought. I suppose it had something to do with the fact that when I was at my desk, I became a different person than the boring one I'd invented for my everyday life. In this sense D.P.

Mere was more than a pseudonym; he was a heteronym with a genuinely independent intellectual life.

A few days later, I packed a bag and made the journey to Cleveland. Only this time, thanks to the small advance from my publisher, I was able to make the trip in a used sedan rather than on a bicycle.

Seventeen

Gwendolyn lived in a mid-century colonial on Lake Erie with her husband and three boys. When she came to the door wearing white slacks and a royal blue blouse, she struck me as an avatar of Ronald Reagan's America. That she had chosen such a conventional suburban life surprised me. Her mantle and walls were decorated with pictures of her husband and three handsome boys, and during a brief tour of her house, I was mystified that she kept no portraits of McKenna hanging on the walls, no magazine covers of the calamitous rocket launch, no condolence letters from Vice President Richard Nixon thanking her for her sacrifice to the country. She invited me to the back patio, where we sat and watched sailboats tacking against the wind. Never entirely comfortable in these stuffy suburban settings, I squirmed in my chair and noticed on the wicker coffee table a copy of my book and a glass ashtray on which lay crossed two neatly rolled joints.

"When you have three teenagers," she said, "you look for ways to take the edge off."

For an hour, we engaged in the obligatory small talk of people who, after a long absence, have become strangers to one another. She told me how she helped manage her husband's orthodontic practice while her boys were at school or playing tennis at the club. In the summer, she spent a lot of time reading. My novel, she told me with a halfhearted laugh, kept her up late at night thinking about the past — and the future. She reached for one of the joints and matches.

"Care for a puff?"

"Had to give it up," I said. "Had to give up a lot of things after my days on the road."

"Suitable material for your next book, I'm sure." She struck a match and lit her aromatic cigarette. "You know, I never thanked you for coming to the Moondog Coronation Ball."

"I've always felt," I said, "that I owed you an apology."

"An apology? For what?"

"I wasn't the right person to call when you needed help."

"Of course you were. Miles always admired you for making the journey. Until then, he never realized just how much grit you had."

Gwendolyn took a modest puff and looked out over the lake.

"I've been meaning to ask you something. Something that has never made a whole lot of sense to me."

"Yes?"

She leaned forward in her chair. "What exactly do you think we saw that night on the reservoir? If it was a meteorite, why didn't anyone else in Heavenly Hill see it? The entire town should have been talking about it. It was as bright as the noonday sun. And when it splashed down, we felt a wave of white heat rolling across the water. You're a science fiction writer. You must have a theory."

I explained how my work couldn't be categorized as science fiction in the strict sense of the term and that the handful of critics who'd bothered to review it considered it "speculative" and not particularly well-written.

"Critics," Gwendolyn said with a dismissive wave of her hand. "I know you're probably sick and tired of people telling you their stories. Everyone thinks their lives would make for a bestseller. But would you mind if I told you a story? One that's hard to explain. What it means, I can't say."

"Of course," I said, genuinely intrigued.

"When I was attending Aspern College, I kept having these awful anxiety dreams. I'd wake up screaming in the middle of the night. I couldn't remember any of these dreams, and I was beginning to frighten my roommate. During the day, things weren't much better. To calm my nerves, I took long walks through the cultural gardens on Rockefeller Drive. Strolled through the museums around University Circle. It didn't seem to help much. I jumped at any sudden sound — a backfiring car, a book falling to the floor. I couldn't eat, couldn't focus on my classes. For a while, I contemplated..."

Her eyes fluttered, and she looked away from me.

"I convinced myself all I needed to do was pop a pill, and everything would magically be okay again. On campus, there were rumors that Mikhaila Zamyatin was experimenting with a new drug that she'd synthesized in her lab."

I recognized the name.

A victim of Stalin's purges and the McCarthy Era witch-hunts, Dr. Zamyatin, professor emeritus at Aspern College and pioneer of quantitative psychology, was a larger-than-life personality who disapproved of alcohol and tobacco use but allowed herself a "devious dram of scotch" during public lectures and puffed cigarettes from a fashionable ivory holder. She'd also garnered notoriety for her controversial lab work with primates and human subjects.

"I was desperate for peace of mind," Gwendolyn continued, "so I went to the doctor's basement lab in Clairmont Hall and enrolled in one of her double-blind studies. A graduate assistant took down my medical information and told me to have a seat in one of the recliners, forming a circle in the middle of the room. Reminded me of Mr. Watts' bible study on the square. There were twelve of us, I think. Most were probably there for the one-hundred-dollar stipend. When Dr. Zamyatin came in, she tried to dispel the rumors about her new wonder drug. She knew most young people were allergic to the idea of the metaphysical and told us the effects of her drug were purely physiological. It lowered lactic acid levels in the blood and stimulated the cerebral cortex to create relaxation and well-being. It was also, she claimed, a kind of truth serum. But subjects didn't speak the truth in the ordinary sense of the word. Rather, the truth spoke to them. About a great many things."

Gwendolyn leaned back and gripped the arms of her chair as if reliving the experience.

"Her assistant gave us each a glass of water and a small paper cup with a pill. At first, nothing happened. I assumed I'd been given a placebo. But after thirty minutes, I saw vivid colors and geometric shapes. Then, the shapes coalesced into a familiar image, a recognizable scene. I knew it was all a hallucination, but I swear it felt just as real as the conversation we're having right now."

Her face changed in some indefinable way, and I no longer recognized the expression she wore.

"The whole experience felt like a chapter from your novel. Or a vision of the future. Suddenly, I wasn't in a lab anymore but driving my brother's '57 Plymouth Fury. I was timid, quiet, terrified of life. You sat in the passenger seat, my trusty copilot, reassuring me that all was well. But instead of a man, you were a woman, a very assertive one who published gritty crime dramas rather than science fiction stories. McKenna sat in the backseat, but now, instead of a dog, he was a mischievous little boy with a ray-gun, shooting out the window at squirrels and chipmunks. We also had a robot that looked like one of those orbs you describe in your book — squishy and opaque with the consistency of a jellyfish. It pulsated like a beating heart and guided us back to Heavenly Hill.

"When we reached my house, McKenna jumped from the car. He was excited to show us how the government had drained the lake. He told me to follow him along a trail into a wooded valley as deep as a canyon. We walked for miles until we came to a circular clearing full of wildflowers where a meteor must have landed. In the center of the clearing was a silver saucer. It looked like a spaceship from one of those B movies when we were kids.

McKenna pointed and told me to board the 'Mothership.' Even though I knew there was a good chance I'd never return to Earth, I walked up the gangway and stepped through the open door."

Gwendolyn grew quiet then and, with a trembling hand, crushed the joint in the ashtray.

"I'm not sure what I was expecting. To find myself standing inside some kind of high-tech time machine, I suppose. Instead, I felt weightless, like I'd slipped from the clumsy machinery of my own body. I floated like a leaf in the wind. I kept floating higher and higher until I passed through the roof of the spaceship and then into the sky. Suddenly, I was surrounded by stars. The Earth looked like just another speck of light. I sped around the galaxy's perimeter, traveling from one star system to the next. I saw a cluster of galaxies, then clusters of clusters. Then I drifted away from the universe altogether and entered a vast darkness. But I wasn't in a void, not exactly. More like a place of quiet rejuvenation. A field of infinite potential, unrestrained creativity. At any second, something new and exciting might pop into existence."

Gwendolyn studied her hands and then looked at me with a level stare.

"In that impenetrable darkness, I sensed a presence — a loving mother, a river, an ocean, an eternal thinking machine, God, someone who walked with God. I don't know what. But I remember crying like a child. And as it drew closer to me, the being's eyes fluttered open as if waking from a deep sleep and regarded me with an expression of compassion and gentle humor.

I'll always remember that look. I'll never forget it. And an instant before I was pulled back into the laboratory, I heard a familiar voice say to me, 'For whom were you crying?'"

Eighteen

While participating in that highly dubious experiment at Aspern College, Gwendolyn Greene was transported to another dimension no scientist could adequately explain. After all, how could someone like Dr. Zamyatin propose to "measure" thoughts and feelings when she didn't understand the phenomenon of consciousness? What *is* consciousness? What is the structure of the soul? What is the mathematical model of the spirit, its desires, its virtues? Maybe the mind isn't a *thing* at all, a quantifiable object that obeys the rules of physics.

Shielded by their status and authority, academics employed by the Department of Measurable Outcomes can't bear anything that challenges their axioms and prejudices. By declaring matter to be the building blocks of reality, they mistake themselves for metaphysicians. But what if consciousness, not matter, is the fundamental stuff of which the universe is made? Obsessed with their dead-end methodologies, scientists fall prey to the pernicious doctrine of cause-and-effect and attempt to reduce the world and everything in it to *stuff*. In doing so, they eradicate all traces of anything recognizably human from the pages of their heavily footnoted books and journals. There is a paradox here. The only reason scientists can be sure of anything at all is because they are conscious beings.

Although we never met again after that afternoon on her back patio, Gwendolyn and I kept in touch. She wrote letters of congratulations whenever I published a new book, and on her birthday, I always had a bouquet of white roses and baby's breath delivered to her house. When I bought my A-frame cabin overlooking Lost Village Lake, she sent a lovely housewarming gift — a porcelain figurine of a boy and girl in a rowboat, a dog standing at attention at the bow.

Ten years ago, when I heard about Gwendolyn's death from the same disease that claimed her mother, I sat in stunned silence at my front window and stared for hours at the lake. Unable to bear the image of Gwendolyn languishing in a clinic after sustaining a traumatic head injury, I left my cabin and wandered the lonely country lanes. I eventually found myself standing in front of her house, now the property of a young couple I'd never met, and stood where the historical marker stands today. I recalled the summer afternoon when Gwendolyn came racing from her front door to show me her new puppy. She cradled McKenna in her arms, all bundled up like a baby in a blanket. Her mother and father sat on the porch and laughed when Gwendolyn rolled in the tall grass and let McKenna tug at her shirt. A sacred image of which I was a blessed witness.

Today, students studying animal intelligence might find a sentence or two about McKenna in history books and scientific journals, but of course, it's Laika that the world remembers. Days after the failed launch in November 1957, the Soviets announced that they'd been victorious in putting a dog into low Earth orbit, but in the decades that followed, it seemed not to matter who first accomplished this remarkable feat. The crucial thing, one might argue, was the adversarial relationship between two powerful nations. Conflict fueled progress and innovation. But had McKenna's death changed anything? If so, had the change been meaningful?

I think of him now and then. Yes, there were times when he was frightened — by the vacuum, the hissing geese, the sharp crack of thunder as a summer storm swept across the lake — but he was a brave little dog, a good boy, and Gwendolyn was always there to comfort him.

An old man now, I rarely pass the Greene house these days, and I haven't gone rowing on the lake in many years. I still tinker with my fiction and have the newsletter to keep me busy. Just last week, I reported how the state, rather than make expensive repairs to the enormous hydroelectric dam and its aging valves, intends to drain the reservoir and restore the valley's original habitat. A pity. Lost Village Lake looks dazzling these days, the zebra mussels having completed their work at long last. Still, I wonder what the conservationists will discover down there, buried in the muck. Maybe they'll excavate the old canal town, the rotted rooftop of its heretical church dotted with dark mollusk shells. Or maybe they'll stumble upon something that defies description, something not made by human hands. Submerged for the better part of a century, a dazzling silver saucer may rise from the fevered swamp.

"Some things should remain mysteries," Gwendolyn told me as we said our final goodbyes.

"You may not know what your book means, but I do. For a lot of years, I tried to forget all about that teenage girl from Heavenly Hill. But then I read your novel and remembered who I truly am. Tonight, I'll sit outside and watch the stars, a woman stranded on a rock spinning around a spherical fire. I've learned to accept that there are things in this world we were never meant to understand, but the stars are no less beautiful because of that. In fact, I think they're more beautiful because of it. Life used to fill me with dread and unease. Now it fills me with wonder. And that's what you've given back to me after such a long time. A sense of wonder."

Grateful to have helped in some small way, I hugged her and then drove away. Somehow, I knew I would see her again, if not in this world, then in another. Lifetime after lifetime. But these are deep matters that I don't pretend to understand, and as the curious Traveler already knows, these words do not appear on the historical marker bearing Gwendolyn's name.

Second Trip

Hilda Whitby and the
Heavenly Light of 1857

Nineteen

A week after the fire claimed her grown son and English Setter, her horses and wagons, her rifles and ledgers, her precisely calibrated lab instruments, and her private library with its glass cabinets and shelves lined with hundreds of notebooks in which she'd meticulously recorded her experimental chemical formulae, Hilda Whitby stood with her back to the river and surveyed for a final time the scorched two-acre parcel where the house, barn, and lumber mill once stood. The elms had burned, too, and the cottonwoods and the reeds that grew in great profusion along the river. Despite the warm weather, she wore a heavy cotton dress that reached to her ankles, one of the few garments that had survived the explosion and the one she'd worn to the funeral services. To the leather leg strap under her skirts, she fastened a dissection knife salvaged from the smoldering heap of timber beams and trusses that once served as her laboratory. The six-inch blade might prove useful should she happen upon one of the saboteurs or highwaymen known to roam the locks after sundown. There had been serious strife in recent days. Railroad workers were arriving by the hundreds to lay the new track that, in another year or two, would render the canal all but obsolete. Unwilling to accept such rapid modernization, some boatmen and laborers had resorted to violence. Just last month, while fishing on the river, a boy found the swollen body of a missing railroad surveyor. The coroner's inquest showed the man had been speared through the back with a canal boat captain's twelve-foot iron-shod setting pole.

Now, using the same horse blanket she'd been beating with a riding crop outside the stable moments before the explosion, Hilda bundled a canteen, a change of clothes, and adequate provisions for a journey of three or four days. Into a pocket sewn inside her bodice, she slipped a pipe and a pouch of tobacco purchased from the general store. After twenty-five years of abstinence, she'd started smoking again. Without the faintest idea of where she might go, she slung the blanket over her shoulder and began walking south along the towpath. She limped as she walked, her right leg having been grazed by toppling masonry when she charged into her lab and tried to rescue her son from the flames.

She didn't dwell for long on the scandal her sudden absence was sure to create. To avoid any awkward encounters in town, she climbed the winding trail behind her property. By then, the morning mist had already lifted, and from a ridge overlooking the valley, she could see the headstones in the churchyard and the stooped silhouettes of her neighbors as they toiled in the fields. She paused to take in an unobstructed view of the canal. It connected dozens of frontier outposts and mist-shrouded hamlets, creating the first direct route between Lake Erie and the Ohio River. A marvel of modern engineering, or so she once believed. Now she regarded the canal as an unsightly scar maliciously carved into the valley's delicate spine.

In a futile effort to widen the canal, allowing for more boat traffic, hundreds of laborers drove their pickaxes and shovels through layers of shale and into unyielding limestone. Grotesquely muscled, painfully thin, their ribs protruding in dark stripes across their bare torsos, the men waded waist-deep through the narrow trench, hauling buckets of black sludge from the bottom. Teams of half-starving mules carried away cartloads of fossilized plants and animals. Things of unknown origin, of incalculable age, of deepest mystery.

Rather than endure the torment of stuffing her swollen and blistered feet into her boots, Hilda went barefoot in the style of the laborers and soon learned to tolerate the sharp sting of stones grinding into her heels and wedging between her toes. She no longer wore the borrowed black veil she'd donned when she'd marched into the engraver's workshop and accused him of having deliberately mangled the epitaph on her boy's slate headstone. She'd wanted it to read

Gareth Whitby
b. 1827 – d. 1857
What we know is very little, but what
we are ignorant of is immense.

Instead, Mr. Clairmont had chiseled the words, *Those who are ignorant of the Lord know very little.* Without paying her the common courtesy of setting aside his hammer and chisel, the engraver sighed with obvious displeasure, bent over a marble slab, and swept away a pyramid of dust from the delicate lips of a half-finished cherub.

"May I remind you, Ms. Whitby, that the markers by which I earn my living stand in a Christian cemetery, not on a pedestal outside some heathen temple or university library."

After a heated exchange, in which Hilda calmly assured him that she would be leaving the premises with a full refund, even if it meant borrowing a pair of his pliers to pull the two gold teeth from his yammering mouth, Mr. Clairmont walked over to the counter and begrudgingly counted out three dollars and fifty cents. Presently, it was the only cash she carried on her person.

Having walked now for more than ten miles, Hilda no longer thought of the headstone or the ongoing investigation surrounding her son's death. She no longer thought of anything at all. Brought on perhaps by the irregular rhythm of her footfalls, she entered into a trance. Her body felt light, her mind free from grief and fear. She continued walking until sundown, a lone figure with a distinctive limp, and then made the gradual descent into the river valley to seek shelter for the night.

Twenty

Bracing herself for the customary crude jokes and muttered propositions, Hilda entered a derelict camp next to a canal lock under construction. The few laborers who could read and write removed their hats after she introduced herself. They'd seen her name in the newspapers and, in solemn tones, offered their condolences. A few rebuked her for her act of bravery, extraordinary though it was. She was fortunate, they said, not to have been pinned beneath the falling timbers and burned alive. These well-meaning remarks Hilda ignored with grace. She accepted their hospitality of food and drink and, as she smoked her pipe around the campfire, listened to the laborers speak of their own misfortunes. They'd come from every state and territory searching for work and now regaled her with the myths and legends of their homes in the mountains and prairies. Like her, they had their share of personal demons, but when they passed the bottle her way, Hilda found she still possessed enough willpower to say no.

A man they called Stanislas sat beside her and topped off his tin cup. A pitiable creature if she'd ever seen one. He looked vaguely reptilian, prehistoric, Mesozoic, a plucked bird in need of basting. Already balding in his youth, he turned his small, close-set eyes to the fire and told her how he'd spent his childhood on a dismal little rock pile in the middle of Lake Erie. Thirty cabins crammed along a single street of mud. A schoolhouse that never opened. A saloon that never closed. A lighthouse, a church, a jail. An island whose secrets were as flat and featureless as the lake on a gray November day. The same island where Gareth's father and namesake had lived as a boy. Perhaps they'd been neighbors, friends, mortal enemies. All of them at once. Hilda said nothing of this and took in his tale.

"Sailors," he said, "tell of flying machines that visit the island when the lake is calm and the sky clear. Electric skyships, they call them. No one knows their origin or purpose. On our island, they disappeared into the caves along the cliff walls. My mother loved to walk along those cliffs. Stared for hours at the moonlit waves. Listened to the surf crashing against the rocks. But she always warned us to watch for the Travelers. During the day, she said, they rested inside the caves and plotted their nightly mischief."

Stanislas leaned forward, his high, shining forehead red in the firelight. He withdrew a silver chain from his coat pocket and thumbed its small anchor as he might a set of prayer beads.

"Early one morning, on their way down to their skiffs and dinghies, the fishermen heard my mother's screams. Not the usual sorts of screams they heard behind closed doors. Not the screams she made when the old man, stinking of whisky from the night before, climbed out of bed and batted her ears for not having a hot breakfast ready for him. My father was a brutal man, have no doubt. A courageous one as well. Survived winter gales on the lake. Nearly froze to death when his boat capsized a mile offshore. Lost a finger. Lost a toe. What choice did he have? We were always hungry. But there was no mistaking the terror the fishermen saw in his eyes. My mother ran from the cabin in her nightdress, the only one she owned, always dirty from shoveling coal into the fire. When she was calm enough to speak, she kept whispering the same words. The Travelers. The Travelers."

Stanislas rocked on his haunches, his left eye starting to twitch, and dragged his fingers through his thinning hair.

"My little sister was missing. She was only five. I was seven. We slept in the same bed at the back of the cabin. Where she'd gone, I couldn't say, no matter how hard my father twisted my ear. Neighbors poured from their cabins. Women, children. The young, the old. We looked under every jetty and inside every vessel. An hour later, the constable came riding into town. Someone must have summoned the law. Not because they suspected my mother of any wrongdoing but because they held a grudge against her. Wanted to see her suffer. People can be like that, you know. Resentments last a long time."

Hilda nodded. She knew exactly what he meant.

Stanislas let the anchor swing in wide flashing arcs from his right hand.

"The constable prided himself on his education. Claimed to have studied law and forensic science by post, and he didn't put much stock in the superstitions of a fisherman's wife. When he finished his interrogation, he stood outside our door. Announced to everyone that a heinous crime had taken place. It took three men to wrestle her to the ground and hogtie her. You might think a boy my age might start to cry, seeing his mother treated that way, but the creature I saw hissing and thrashing in the mud looked nothing at all like the woman I knew. Even after they tossed her into the back of the constable's wagon, she kept screaming about a luminous disc that came screaming from the stars. Hovered over the village, she said, and cast a blinding beam through our cabin window."

Stanislas' small, raspy voice had worked its way into an agitated squeak.

"My little girl has been summoned! She's been summoned!"

He took a deep breath, his hands shaking so badly now that he nearly dropped the rattling chain into the fire.

"The neighbors looked away, pretended not to understand. But we all knew what she meant. No one, not even my father, spoke a word in her defense. She's still alive, last I heard, locked up in a clinic in Cleveland. Doctors there use the latest scientific treatments. Pills. Injections. Electric shocks. Sophisticated brain therapies."

The men rolled their cigarettes and swatted the mosquitoes that made so many of them ill. Just today, there were rumors of another severe outbreak of swamp fever one hundred miles south of the lock.

For a long time, no one spoke. Then, to break the silence, the bull cook asked Hilda where she was heading. The men knew she was once a woman of considerable means and might wish to employ the services of an armed escort. She thanked them but declined their generous offers even as they competed to underbid one another. After saying goodnight, Hilda stood up, brushed dust and ash from her skirt, and wandered off to a relatively quiet corner of the camp. For the camps were never entirely quiet, and certainly not on this night as it was payday and the gamblers, slugging back jars of rotgut whisky, tried to triple their wages.

On a small patch of trampled grass, Hilda wrapped herself in the rough blanket and gazed at the spinning constellations. She wondered what lurked among the stars and the vast spaces in between. Why had the Travelers come all this way? Were they, too, on some kind of quest? Over the years, while working in the solitude of her laboratory on her failed experiments, she had intuited that the entire universe was not, as her scientific contemporaries suspected, mindless and mechanistic but was, from its very origins, imbued with an intelligence that far surpassed anything the human mind could hope to comprehend.

She had only just closed her eyes, Stanislas' strange story blending into dream, when she felt a cold hand crawling across her shoulder and down to the small of her back. Hilda, breathing lightly, remained motionless and then, in one swift motion, withdrew the knife from under her skirt. By then, the camp was a pandemonium of screeching fiddles and bare-knuckled brawls, and no one heard the wretched howls when she plunged the knife deep into a thrusting bare buttock.

Her assailant stumbled into the shadows, a whimpering apparition yanking up his threadbare britches. Hilda climbed unsteadily to her feet and straightened her skirt. As she dragged her blanket closer to the fire, she found, wedged in the ground near her feet, a silver anchor affixed to a chain. After she wiped the blood-splattered blade across the grass, she grabbed the charm and slipped it into her pocket. She didn't notice that her tobacco pouch was missing until noon the next day when she felt a headache coming on, but by then, she'd already traveled a dozen miles from the camp.

She kept a steady pace, knowing it was only a matter of time before the law began to search for her.

Twenty-One

Three days later, just as her feet were finding a natural rhythm and her badly bruised leg was beginning to heal, Hilda decided against her better judgment to accept a ride in a covered wagon from a self-proclaimed apothecary traveling under the name Professor Sharpwater. During her three decades at the mill, Hilda had encountered many such rascals. In good weather and bad, they came hauling heavy wagonloads of useless trinkets. Always dressed in flamboyant outfits better suited for the stage than the frontier, they stood on boxes and, with their carefully rehearsed speeches, tried to sell at extravagant prices exotic salves and elixirs from the Far East or the latest gadgets guaranteed to make life more convenient for pioneer families — calibrated scales, electric batteries, a wheeled machine with rotating blades that cut grass. She'd seen matches, too, boxes of them. Dried blobs of antimony sulfide and potassium chlorate at the tips of short, wooden sticks. An idea so obvious that Hilda berated herself for not having thought of it.

Above the sound of clinking bottles, Professor Sharpwater told her how he'd just returned from Europe, where, for the better part of a year, he'd studied alchemy and the dark arts under the watchful gaze of a famous Swiss physician. Hilda resisted the urge to roll her eyes and noticed the coiled snake tattooed on the man's right wrist.

"My mentor," he said, "lived in a stone house on the shores of a beautiful lake. Built it with his own hands. In his library, under lock and key, he kept papyrus scrolls of great antiquity written in Latin, Greek, Hebrew, and Sanskrit. It was from these ancient writings that I learned the secrets of my trade. And what, precisely, *is* my trade?"

He opened the wooden crate at his feet, reached a hand under the lid, and produced a small bottle filled with black liquid.

"This, madam, is a refreshing tonic of carbonated water and pure cane sugar with beneficial additives from the sacred forest you see all around you. Sacred because, once distilled, these additives release a powerful spirit, so say the Wyandot medicine men in these parts. A spirit that gives to all who drink it a remarkable burst of energy."

He handed her the bottle and tipped his wide-brimmed hat.

"With my compliments, Ms...."

"Whitby." She held the bottle to her lips and then stopped. "This isn't liquor, is it?"

"Not at all, Ms. Whitby. Unlike liquor, my tonic brightens the humors and sharpens the senses, not dulls them. But as I am an honest man, I must warn you that it may prove habit-forming. People who enjoy one bottle crave another and another."

Parched after such a long walk under the hot sun, Hilda uncorked the bottle and took an experimental sip.

"Sweet," she said, her eyes growing wide.

Although it was foolish to trust the nonsensical blather of a man who, in all likelihood, was peddling poison, she emptied the bottle in a single, breathless gulp. She touched her stomach, clutched the wagon's splintered side, and let out a belch that echoed through the valley.

"Oh, my..."

Professor Sharpwater slapped his knee. "That's the carbonation talking, a relatively new invention, new at least to this part of the world. In Geneva, my mentor bottled seltzer at a handsome profit. I'm delighted to say I'm the first of his disciples to bring it this far west."

"Makes my heart race," Hilda said, wiping her mouth with the back of her hand.

"The pawpaw's effects are readily felt."

He took the bottle from her and placed it in the crate with a dozen other empties that rattled and clanked as the wagon jounced along the path.

"The secret is in the fermentation process. It unlocks properties similar to those of the coca leaf found in Peru. Several years ago, while selling seltzer sweetened with simple cane sugar, I found myself conducting a business transaction with the owners of a traveling show. Wizards and dragons and knights in shining armor. I met all manner of strange show folk, among them a witch doctor who taught me the secrets of the pawpaw. You may dismiss his claims, madam, as the superstitions of a savage, but keep in mind that his people have inhabited this valley for untold centuries and have acquired a deep understanding of its plants and their medicinal properties. After performing a ritual dance for the crowd, the witch doctor invited me to his tent to share a cup of tea made from the juice and crushed leaves of the fruit. After a few sips, I had a sudden flash of insight, a vision, you might say, in which I saw how the distillation process could be used to help my fellow travelers. Some medicines heal the body. Others heal the mind. But a rare few, like the pawpaw, have the miraculous power to heal the soul."

Accustomed to the valley's tranquility, Hilda hadn't realized until this moment just how annoying the sound of a human voice could be. She followed the trajectory of a hawk across the sky and dreamed of flying away.

"So potent is its life-giving energy that you may feel inspired to unhitch my old mare and pull this wagon by yourself to the next village. If only the engineers and foremen would buy my product by the barrel, they could keep the gandy dancers working at maximum efficiency and complete the new railroad by the end of next year. Unfortunately, quantities of my product are limited to what I can transport along this primitive towpath. Ah, but once the railroad is open, I'll be able to move hundreds of crates across the state by steam locomotive. Truly a wonder of modern science, the iron dragon..."

He trailed off and turned to Hilda as if noticing his passenger for the first time.

"Whitby did you say?" The man's eyes drifted to her ragged dress and filthy feet. "Any relation to those folks who operated that sawmill up north?"

"No," Hilda stated flatly.

"Well, thank goodness for that. Terrible tragedy."

"Oh?"

"You don't read the papers, I take it?"

"I can't read."

"A pity. Good books, Ms. Whitby, make for fine companions. And they never fail to keep a restless mind occupied on rainy days."

Hilda smoothed her skirts, her body trembling slightly from the man's potent tonic, and continued to stare straight ahead. The towpath seemed to stretch on forever, and she worried they wouldn't reach the nearest town until after sunset.

"According to the newspapers, the woman who owned the mill read a great many books. Her knowledge of natural philosophy was formidable. The authorities believe she may have been in possession of illegal and extremely combustible substances. How else to explain the explosion and why the fire burned so fiercely, so *unnaturally?* And for so many hours? Flattened everything. The grist and stables. And the birds, Ms. Whitby. The charred remains of so many birds. Hundreds of them. A curiosity. Lucrative business reduced to ashes. And a son dead. Her only child. Perhaps it's in bad taste to speak idly of such things, Ms. Whitby, but the woman wasn't married. She'd *never* been married. Didn't seem to bother her in the least. Neighbors say it was almost a point of pride with her, not that their gossip should have any bearing on her legal defense."

"Legal defense?" Hilda asked.

"Well, yes. The woman is wanted for questioning. The authorities are no longer calling it an act of God. This was no lightning strike as originally believed. No, this was a scientific experiment gone terribly wrong."

A curious sense of paranoia came over Hilda. These charlatans could spin a fantastic tale to suit any circumstance, and she suspected Professor Sharpwater, with his scuffed suede hat and worn white gloves, of embellishing the newspaper accounts. She knew all of their tricks. Make the customer feel slightly unsettled, vulnerable, at their mercy.

"You're familiar, I take it, with the destructive power of the new explosives the railroads are using to blast through granite? There may come a time, and not long from now, when some misguided scientist learns to distill gunpowder and create a weapon with enough explosive power to level an entire city. You may laugh, Ms. Whitby, but it wouldn't surprise me if this woman was working for the government. Developing top-secret chemical agents. Depend upon it, madam. Those warmongers in Washington have no compunction about testing such weapons on an unsuspecting population. We all know about the evils of tobacco and alcohol, but what about ideas?"

"Ideas?"

Professor Sharpwater leaned toward her and spoke at a low pitch, as if communicating some private message.

"It occurred to me, Ms. Whitby, that ideas can be distilled into something just as potent as whisky and gin. Take cash money, for instance, or political parties. Or religious beliefs. Forgive me for speaking plainly, but I'm a modern man, a student of the Enlightenment, and I believe our notion of God is simply a useful fiction that we've conjured up and distilled into a convenient explanation for the unsolved mystery of being. In America, we've grown addicted to lucre and the Lord, though most people confuse the two."

With a reproachful grin, Hilda said, "Tell me, sir. Are you a quack? Or a preacher? Or perhaps both?"

Professor Sharpwater shook the reins, and the old Welsh pony went from a trot to a canter. He straightened his back and with a theatrical air of indignation said, "I understand, Ms. Whitby, that people of faith may regard such talk as blasphemous, but I also believe that unkind words can be distilled into disgust, hatred, and violence. Negative emotions coil around a man's heart. They constrict his soul. And with the technologies we currently possess, these dark feelings might prove to be the end of us all. And that is why, Ms. Whitby, my new and improved carbonated tonic is essential. By lifting the human spirit, it may save us from our own worse impulses. And furthermore..."

Twenty-Two

That evening, accompanied by the warble of a long-eared bush owl, they arrived at a trading post near a sharp bend in the river. For a boomtown in midsummer, the streets were eerily quiet. Hilda saw no lantern light in the windows of the clapboard houses that lined the square, and she heard no spirited laughter from the town's only saloon. Expansion of the canal seemed to have been temporarily halted here. Shovels and pickaxes lay scattered in the weeds, and an expensive stump puller was left unattended next to a wheelbarrow overflowing with crushed limestone.

Outside the Copper Penny Guest House, Professor Sharpwater halted his wagon. Even from the street, Hilda could smell the sawdust and overturned spittoons, but she judged the place adequate for an overnight stay. She had little choice in the matter. After listening for hours to the apothecary's lunatic prophecies about government conspiracies and apocalyptic civil wars, she was willing to sleep almost anywhere. Desperate for a moment's peace, Hilda shouldered her bag and hopped from the wagon.

Professor Sharpwater tipped his hat. "A pleasure to make your acquaintance, Ms. Whitby."

Trying to disguise the pain that shot through her leg, Hilda gave a terse salute but did not thank him. She trudged up the steps to the verandah. Behind her, the ungainly wagon clinked and clattered as it rolled away into the night.

Without looking back, Hilda stepped through the double doors. Inside, rifling through the dog-eared pages of an encyclopedia, a girl of about sixteen sat on a bench near the fireplace and watched Hilda cross the parlor. The firelight distorted the girl's sharp features and narrow, green eyes. She looked like an aggressive cat about to pounce on an unsuspecting sparrow.

When he heard the plank floors creak and groan, the innkeeper, nodding off behind the front desk, came awake with a start.

The girl closed her book and placed it on the bench. "Well? Ask the lady if she'd like a room."

Through drooping eyelids, the innkeeper stared blankly at Hilda. He absently adjusted his coat and vest, both of which were missing buttons. After clearing his throat, he said, "Like a room?"

Hilda glanced at the girl before returning her gaze to the man. "Yes, please."

The innkeeper stood motionless, the expression on his ashen face never changing.

The girl sighed. "Now, ask her to sign in."

From his shirt pocket, the innkeeper produced a pair of spectacles. Before putting them on, he used his sleeve to polish the lenses. "You one of the surveyor's wives?"

"She ain't a surveyor's wife." The girl eyed the horse blanket slung over Hilda's shoulder. "She ain't an engineer's wife either. And you! You ain't supposed to make inquiries into a lady's private affairs."

The innkeeper waved a hand, possibly at the girl, more likely at the mosquito brushing against the tip of his nose. He spun the guestbook around and adjusted the knob of the kerosene lamp at the corner of his desk. The flame cast shifting shadows across the ceiling.

"Sign here."

He handed Hilda a quill dipped in ink so old it had turned thick as glue. Her nerves frayed after that interminable wagon ride, she scratched her real name. A careless oversight. She'd intended to use an alias. In the future, she would need to be more cautious.

Suddenly, the girl was standing beside her. A teenager, but the bloom on her cheeks was already fading fast. She placed her calloused hands on the desktop, strands of strawberry blonde hair falling across the nape of her neck, and squinted at the signature.

"Staying with us long … Ms. Whitby?"

"Just the night. I'll be leaving early in the morning."

She gave Hilda a strange, lingering look. "Well, we don't serve breakfast until seven. And you're too late for supper. We closed the kitchen for the night."

Even though she was famished and her rations were running low, Hilda nodded and said, "That's perfectly alright."

The girl snapped her fingers at the innkeeper.

"Don't make the lady carry her bag. Quick, show our guest to her room. Put her in the athenaeum. Convenient access to the washroom across the hall."

She smiled, and Hilda saw a dark gap where one of the girl's incisors was missing.

Mumbling like a sullen child, the innkeeper shuffled from behind the front desk and wrestled the horse blanket from Hilda's shoulder.

"This way."

He strode across the parlor and turned down a dark corridor whose walls desperately needed paint.

"I hope you find everything to your satisfaction," the girl called from the bench. She opened the encyclopedia, and in the firelight, her face seemed to float above the floor.

At the end of the corridor, the innkeeper fingered through his heavy ring.

"No reason for her to keep this room locked," he said, more to himself than to Hilda. "Ah, here it is!"

After struggling with the lock, he kicked open the door with one unlaced boot and tossed her blanket to the sawdust floor. He lit a lamp hanging by a hook above the four-poster bed.

Startled by what she saw inside, Hilda hesitated in the doorway.

The innkeeper snorted. "Yes, she's a strange one, that imp. Whenever she has a dollar in her pocket, she spends it on books. Dictionaries, almanacs, histories, manifestos. Lots of novels. Trashy ones, mainly. Reads the bible, too. But I doubt the heavenly gates will open for a ferocious hellcat such as she." He glanced over his shoulder and whispered, "If she doesn't have a dollar in her pocket, she steals books. I believe it's a kind of sickness. More dangerous than the fever going around."

Afraid to touch anything for fear that she might be buried alive, Hilda reluctantly entered the room and skirted the teetering stacks that lined the walls, a number of volumes that easily rivaled those in her laboratory.

"She don't read the books for pleasure," the innkeeper continued. "No, she studies them. Studies their patterns. Says the patterns are predictable. As regular as the seasons. The other day, I caught her reading a love manual. From ancient India. Lots of pictures in it. Pictures of men and women." The innkeeper began to giggle. "The imp says it teaches ladies how to tolerate re-*pug*-nant partners. You know what that word means? Re-*pug*-nant?"

"Extremely distasteful."

Hilda stepped around the innkeeper, trying not to brush against him, and tested the thin mattress.

"Your daughter," she said, "has a sharp tongue."

"Daughter?" The innkeeper's smile faded. "The imp ain't my *daughter*."

"I do apologize. From the familiar way she spoke to you, I was given to believe…"

"Ain't my daughter." He closed the curtains and focused his eyes on the floor. "You'll be wanting a bath, I suppose. I'll fill the tub. Your dress and underthings. Give 'em over. I'll wash them for you."

"Thank you, but I prefer to go straight to bed."

"The imp is particular about the bedding. Doesn't want it soiled. Now off with that dirty dress."

"You may leave now."

"No need to raise your voice." The innkeeper hurried to the door. "Just be sure to blow out that lamp before you fall asleep. The imp doesn't like it when guests burn oil all night. Oil costs money. And no smoking in bed!" He swiveled sharply on his heels and, before slamming shut the door, said, "If you need anything, I'll be at the front desk."

Hilda reached into a pocket and ran her fingers along the chain and anchor, a reminder of the dangers she'd already faced on the road and might face again. Crossing the room to bolt the door, she perused some of the titles. *In Remembrance of a Weeping Queen, Lady Cordelia's Prison of Wishes, Madame La Roche's Essays in Idleness.* At random, she chose *In The Hours of Affliction: or the Poor Man's Friend,* a medical book that provided step-by-step instructions for performing emergency medical procedures using instruments that one might find in any home. Bloodletting, blistering, teeth pulling, waterboarding. Hilda flinched at the graphic illustrations of mangled hands and broken bones. Then she remembered the knife strapped to her leg and considered operating on herself.

After lowering the flame, she sat on the edge of the bed and gazed at the endless replicas of herself in the triptych of mirrors above a dressing table. From skimming the medical book, she knew where to make a precise incision that would end her suffering and silence the disquieting voices in her head. One swift slash straight across her throat and the rest, as they say, would be silence.

Twenty-Three

She'd grown so accustomed to sleeping on ground baked hard by the summer sun that the stiff mattress felt strangely luxurious, and the moment her head touched the pillow, she fell into a deep sleep.

She found herself standing inside a small workshop behind the mill. Her son, a withdrawn, stoic bachelor tethered to his mother's knee from earliest childhood, found refuge here from his mother's hectoring voice and his responsibilities managing the mill. From time to time a great horned owl appeared on the rooftop. It twisted its head completely around and watched Gareth at work. Transfixed by its stare, her son spoke to the owl, asked it questions, pondered the meaning of its unblinking black eyes and unchanging expression. He sensed its almost sardonic intelligence. "Smarter than any cat or dog," he said. "Smarter than most people."

Inside the workshop, on dozens of large canvases, Gareth painted birds native to the surrounding hills and valleys — yellow warblers, green herons, blue-headed vireos, black-capped chickadees. A perfectionist like his mother, he insisted on getting the details right.

He was also an accomplished taxidermist, and Hilda paused to scrutinize three buzzards gazing down at her from wood perches drilled into walls. The creatures mystified her. Every March 15th, the buzzards returned after a long winter absence to the surrounding meadows. They swept down from gloomy skies and hopped awkwardly through melting snowdrifts. Scavengers without voice boxes, they bullied their way through life with unsettling grunts and hisses and buried their hooked beaks deep in their black feathers. Famished after their journey home, they cleaned up the carcasses in the nearby woods. Nothing remained when they were finished but heaps of bones.

Gareth, examining a fresh specimen, waved his mother over to the table.

They both ignored the black smoke pouring into the workshop from beneath the door and through the open windows.

"I think some sort of magic is involved," he told her. "How else can you explain it? They fly hundreds of miles and return to this precise location on the same date without fail. It isn't chance. It isn't coincidence. Legends say birds serve as the guardians of long-lost boys and girls."

Hilda coughed, waving her hand through the smoke. "Buzzards can't make logical deductions," she said. "They're just mindless machines. Everything that walks and crawls and flies upon this cursed planet is fully automated."

She stepped over to his table, pushing aside his degreasers, dyes, waxes, and mason jars overflowing with glass eyes until she found a pair of sharpened shears and a scalpel.

Ignoring the flames that raced up the walls and across the ceiling, she sliced open the dead buzzard and said, "See! Magic has nothing to do with it. On the inside, birds are nothing but machinery. Machinery without any real meaning and purpose. Just like humans. But who, or what, set the machinery in motion? Now, that's what I'd like to know. I suspect the whole of creation is under the control of an advanced race of scientists and mathematicians who possess godlike intelligence."

"You're wrong, Mother," Gareth said, fire issuing forth from his lips. "We're made of light. A light that burns brightly in the darkness."

By that time, everything was engulfed in flames. Hilda turned away as the fire consumed her son.

She opened her eyes and suppressed a scream.

Struggling to remember where she was, she sat up in the dark room. She waited for the dream to fade from memory, but the horrible sounds persisted. At first, she thought the obscene cries and feral grunts were part of her nightmare, the death throes of a young man flailing in the fire. She clamped her hands over her ears and buried her face in the pillows, but when the wall began to vibrate, she abandoned all hope of falling back asleep.

Unable to ignore the clinking bottles and squeaking bedsprings coming from the adjacent room, Hilda stumbled through the dark, gathered up her belongings, and hurried out the door.

Twenty-Four

Outside the inn, she saw Professor Sharpwater's wagon tied to the hitching post, the Welsh pony scratching at the dirt and shaking its badly matted mane and tail. The mosquitos were ferocious.

"Decided to switch accommodations?"

The innkeeper, rocking wildly in a chair, followed her with his bulging red eyes. He held a bottle of tonic in one hand, four empties forming a barricade around his spindly legs.

"Won't find another inn until you reach the next county."

Hilda limped down the steps, dropped her bundled blanket in the street, and turned to face him.

"We both know, sir, what kind of establishment you're running here. Exploiting an innocent child for profit."

"Innocent!" He laughed so hard he smashed his head against the wall. "Damn it to hell."

"I should summon the sheriff."

"The sheriff? He's at death's door, poor soul. Like half the people in this town. And innocent ain't the word I'd use to describe an impudent hellcat such as she." The innkeeper rubbed his head and checked his fingertips for blood. "Say, do you think the sheriff would be willing to deputize me? I always wanted to be a lawman. Ever since I was a boy. No one would laugh at me then. No one would dare laugh. Not even the imp!"

He sprang from his chair, knocking over the bottles like a set of dominos, his wretched voice filling the empty streets.

"I'd like to be a bounty hunter. Catching criminals on the run. I'd bring them to justice and watch them hang by the neck." He smacked his lips, wobbled on the balls of his feet, and clutched the handrail for support. "That's damn fine medicine. Got a serious kick to it. Man is a wizard. Think he has more in his wagon?"

"What the *hell* is going on out here?"

Wearing only a nightdress, her skin glistening with sweat, the girl burst from the double doors and jabbed a finger at the innkeeper's chest.

"What is this? Enoch! You take them bottles from the professor's wagon?"

The innkeeper inched away from her and scratched his head.

"We negotiated a deal. Five dollars for the best tonic I ever tasted."

"Five dollars! Damn fool, you ain't got five dollars."

He fumbled with a pouch tied to his waist. "Empty. Better get more cash from the safe."

"Like hell you will. You can't remember the combination anyway."

Hilda, with growing disdain, listened to them argue and then started down the road.

"Just a minute there, Ms. Whitby," the girl called. "We're not running a charity here. You *are* Hilda Whitby, aren't you? I read all about you in the papers. We used to get regular deliveries twice a day, mornings and evenings, until the fever came. Service has been temporarily disrupted. Everything has been disrupted."

The girl leaned against the railing, the orange halo of an oil lamp highlighting wisps of her unruly hair. There was something obscene about the way she leaned against the post, arms crossed, one strap of her nightgown dangling from her exposed shoulder. A backwoods Aphrodite ready for a fistfight, a yellowing bruise above her left breast, her freshly painted lips moist with anticipation.

"Papers say you designed the mill yourself. Say you know mathematical equations and scientific formulas and such. I admire that. I'm self-taught, too. I know addition and subtraction. So the cutpurses round here can't cheat me."

The girl glanced back at the innkeeper, who was now sitting on the steps and using a stick to scrape manure from his boot heels.

"Peabrain here can hardly spell his name. Can't run an inn, that's for sure. Technically, the Copper Penny is still his place, but he can't be left alone. Not for a minute, isn't that so?"

She rapped her fingers on the railing, breaking the man's concentration.

"He's not right, Ms. Whitby. Not after that alpaca kicked him in the head three years ago. Lucky to be breathing, I suppose. He tell you about Abelard?"

The man sniffed the stick and tossed it into the weeds.

"Abelard..." A familiar name from the past, though Hilda couldn't place it.

"That's what we named the dog on account of it was neutered. Some carnival people abandoned him here. You like going to the magic lantern shows, Ms. Whitby? Pictures of lords and ladies and knights in armor?"

"I was never partial to that sort of thing," Hilda answered. "Or to dogs, for that matter."

"Well, this mongrel proved a fine companion. Always sleeping at my feet and following me from room to room. A proud hunter, too. Left gifts for me every morning. Lots of dead chipmunks. Placed them at my feet. Then, one day, Abelard was gone. At first, I didn't think too much of it. But around suppertime, I started to worry. The rat snakes along the canal can get big enough to strangle a dog. Searched all over the guest house. Then I went out back and found this genius pretending to hang sheets on the clothesline. Asked if he'd seen Abelard. But he kept his back to me. Wouldn't look me in the eye."

The innkeeper turned to Hilda. "Don't listen to her," he implored. "I didn't do anything."

"Takes a certain kind of man to harm an animal," the girl said. "Yes, a certain kind of man."

"I tried giving him a bath, was all. Don't listen to her. Abelard was rolling in the mud and horseshit. Paw prints all over our clean floors."

"Since when have you cared about cleanliness?" the girl spat. "I yanked the clothesline off the tree, fresh sheets blowing across the yard and into the street. And you! Your hands and face all scratched to hell. Shirt sleeves shredded. Oh, Ms. Whitby, he looked a sight."

"Giving him a bath was all."

"I found Abelard floating in a steel tub next to the pump. People say he done it on account of his injury. His brain's been turned into a kind of pudding. Can't control himself. I swear, I don't know what you'd do without me. You need round-the-clock supervision. And me, left to do all the serious work around here."

The innkeeper stood up and ambled nonchalantly toward the apothecary's wagon. "A bath..."

"Once the laborers return to dredge the canal," the girl said, "I'm going to have my hands full. Dozens of men, hundreds maybe, back on the job, eager to empty their pockets first chance they get. There's going to be a great deal of money to be made, Ms. Whitby. A great deal of money. I'll be looking for extra hands, if you take my meaning. But you know how it is. One girl shows up at your door, another leaves. They either come with the laborers or run off with them. Makes it difficult to keep a house properly staffed. And I need to be prepared to meet demand."

Hilda planted her hands on her hips. "I beg your pardon?"

The girl laughed and shook her head.

"Oh, I wasn't suggesting ... I hope you didn't think I meant..."

She stepped barefoot from the porch and approached Hilda.

"It's true, Ms. Whitby, some of the degenerates who visit this house have a taste for tough old birds like yourself. But

I had something entirely different in mind. What these girls need is a mother superior who can talk sense to them. Or beat it into them. I thought maybe you could help manage the talent. Keep the new employees in line. I'd be willing to make you an equal partner. We'll split everything down the middle. Now, you won't get an offer like that anywhere else, especially for someone in your predicament."

"My predicament?"

"You're new to the outlaw life, aren't you?" The girl gave Hilda a pitying look. "Papers say your son died a day shy of his thirtieth birthday. Swallowed up in a ball of fire. Did he do much traveling, Ms. Whitby? For business purposes, I mean? Probably I'd recognize him. Seems I've known just about every man who's journeyed along this canal."

"My personal life is of no concern to you."

The girl smiled, her eyes gleaming and aggressive. "There is no private life, Ms. Whitby, not anymore. Not if the newspapers decide to take an interest in you. Your life is a matter of public record now. The law is offering a reward for your known whereabouts. Some advice, Ms. Whitby. When you're on the run, you don't stay in hotels. But have no fear. I won't breathe a word to anyone."

Hilda touched the girl's shoulder. "Thank you, young lady, for your discretion and for the unusual business proposition. But I'm going to pass on your offer. And, if I may, I'd like to offer some advice of my own. In the future, you should apply your knowledge to more noble pursuits."

The girl swatted Hilda's hand away. "I don't pretend to be a lady, Ms. Whitby. And I don't take advice from amateur fugitives."

Hilda picked her blanket off the ground and began walking down the empty street.

"These days, Ms. Whitby, there's not much the newspapers won't print if they think it'll sell copies. They create stories rather than report them. In some ways, I suppose, many editors are running a house not much different from this one. Don't judge us too harshly, Ms. Whitby. Some of us need to make ends meet any way we can. And you? Don't you need to eat like the rest of us? How will you earn your keep when everyone thinks you're on the run?"

The innkeeper, opening crates and shaking empty bottles at the back of Professor Sharpwater's wagon, waved to Hilda as she passed.

"Where you going? Nothing but wilderness that way."

Ignoring him, Hilda plodded into the darkness beyond the lonely ring of light. Before vanishing down the trail, she turned to look back at the girl standing outside the Copper Penny and saw Professor Sharpwater hovering in the front window, a troubled look on his face.

Twenty-Five

She felt the fever coming on late the following day.

Dehydrated and blinded by the relentless sun, Hilda staggered from the shade of an old-growth forest and skirted a vast beaver marsh covered with flowering water lilies. In this part of the valley, the canal had fallen into disuse, and the towpath tapered away to a poorly maintained trail. On a mossy log, a family of curious muskrats observed her clumsy progress. Blue-tipped dragonflies buzzed her head before darting into the reeds. Hilda, swinging wildly at them, smashed her bare toes against the thick roots of an oak and fell so hard that she tore her dress at the knees. When the pain finally subsided, she knelt beside the marsh and, using a cloth bag as a filter, squeezed water into a cupped hand. At the mill, she'd designed a sand filtration column to purify their water supply, but on the road, she had to make do with the rudimentary tools she carried. Her muscles aching and sweat stinging her eyes, Hilda decided to rest a moment on her blanket.

When she awoke an hour later, she felt cold raindrops pelting her cheeks. In the cattails, the low drone of courting bullfrogs nearly drowned out the deep rumbles of an advancing summer storm. She sat up and saw a seething wall of dark clouds pressing down on the valley's southern ridge. They cast a sickly green glow over the wetland. During her years at the mill, Hilda had witnessed her share of flash floods and knew she had minutes to seek higher ground. She struggled to her feet and hurried along the path.

Ever since leaving the inn, she hadn't seen a soul, but now she thought she heard footsteps behind her and thin, mocking laughter. Hilda spun around and fumbled for the knife strapped to her leg. If only she'd rescued one of her carbine rifles from the fire.

"I haven't any money if robbery is your intention!"

She wondered if the girl or innkeeper had given her up to a bounty hunter now tracking her along the canal.

"I'm armed! Do you hear me?"

More laughter. And crackling leaves in the underbrush. This time much closer.

"If you're the law, you need to identify yourself."

At that instant, the temperature plummeted, and everything became eerily still. Hilda made no attempt to move. Her mind raced with images. Capture and imprisonment. A trial. An unsympathetic judge. A jury lusting for retribution as they might against a witch known to brew lethal potions and cast powerful spells. From the courtroom window, she would have an unobstructed view of the gallows, the noose, the jeering mob. Before the execution, the constable would parade her before the press to record her final pleas for mercy. "My son's death was an accident! I'm innocent!" Afterward, medical students would perform a post-mortem to look for signs of abnormalities in her brain and spleen.

Now, abandoning her blanket in the briars, Hilda ran from the trail and into the brush. Prickly pear cactuses slashed her arms and ankles, and she found herself trapped in a dense thicket of buckthorn. Bleeding and feverish, she fought her painful way to a clearing and slumped against the knotted trunk of a solitary willow. A bitterly cold wind swept through the sedges and switchgrass. The first fat raindrops struck the leaves. Within seconds, shallow streams formed on the hard ground and coursed through the dead summer grass.

In the brush, mere feet from where she sat, something growled and crouched low to the ground, its eyes flashing with each crack of lightning.

The rain came in earnest now, a torrential downpour that stung her lacerated arms and legs. Her heavy black dress soaked and stinking, Hilda gripped the tree and, shivering uncontrollably, pulled herself up. She shrank from the deafening boom of a nearby lightning strike, more terrifying by far than any laboratory mishap. The great danger now, she knew, came from positive charges climbing from the ground and forming streamers.

Through a curtain of rain, an animal padded into the clearing. It flicked water from its tail and paced back and forth in front of the tree. Hilda pressed her back against the trunk, her hands trembling so badly that she dropped the knife. She'd seen large coyotes before, and ten years ago, she'd spotted what must have been one of the last dire wolves trekking across the Ohio snowfields. But she'd never encountered an animal so aggressive as this one. She feared she'd stumbled too close to its den and litter of whining pups. She still had a few provisions left in her pockets, small chunks of dried meat, a piece of stale bread wrapped in paper. Maybe if she left them here, the creature, whatever it was, would leave her alone.

The indistinct figure panted and sniffed. It scratched the ground with its hind legs.

Somehow, Hilda intuited that it meant her no harm and wished for her to follow it.

Keeping a safe distance, she left the clearing and fought her way back to the muddy trail. The animal led her to the valley wall and along a series of steep switchbacks. Unable to find her footing, she slipped on the slick shale and slid backward. Her face planted in the stones, her fingers clawing at the crumbling rocks, she turned in time to see a sycamore one hundred feet tall break loose from a sandstone boulder and sail down the slope into the canopy below. By then, the valley had become a roiling river of black mud that swept away everything in its path — trees, plants, pulverized deadwood, the jumbled bones of pack animals destined to leave another deposit in the unfathomably ancient limestone cliffs.

Hilda kept moving.

Near the eastern ridge, a powerful gust nearly dislodged her from a wide ledge that cantilevered over the valley floor. The animal, veiled by sheets of rain, watched her from a cave entrance, its eyes burning in the dark. Hilda peered inside. Within its purgatorial darkness, she detected a distant circle of firelight. Accepting whatever fate awaited her, she crawled away from the unforgiving rain and through the narrow opening. When her eyes adjusted to the gloom, she saw embedded in the rockface a gigantic, fossilized fish. It threatened to snap its jaws shut when she reached out a hand to trace its thousand jagged teeth. Other shapes were trapped in the stone — horn coral, mollusk shells, a colony of antennaed creatures that looked equal parts lobster, scorpion, and cockroach.

"Come," said a voice, "sit by the fire and warm your hands."

She squinted and realized that what she thought was a dog was, in fact, a middle-aged man, his matted hair reaching down to his shoulders. Even without his tarnished shield and armor, Hilda recognized him at once.

"Abelard?" she whispered. "I haven't seen you since…"

"Ah, so you *do* remember me."

She approached the fire and stretched out her hands. "Is this a place where people come to die?"

"Not exactly." He pulled a piece of birch from the fire and held it high above his head like a torch. The cave seemed to go on forever. "It's where people come to complete their quest."

"I'm not on a quest," Hilda said, her teeth chattering.

"You've been on a quest for a long time now. Longer than you can possibly imagine. You've just forgotten."

"No, you're mistaken. I'm not looking for anything. But I suspect some people are looking for me."

Abelard smiled. "Perhaps it would be easier for me to show you."

He stood up and, without waiting for her, strode along a passageway of twisting stone.

She warily rose to her feet and followed. Together, they traversed an alien world of glistening stalagmites and flowstone. They crossed a natural bridge with a gaping abyss on either side and then made their way through a disorienting labyrinth. Hilda felt trapped, the smooth stone walls narrowed and expanded and then narrowed again until they seemed to converge and threaten to crush her. At last, the tapering passages opened to a cathedral-like chamber buttressed by great limestone columns. Painted on its enormous walls were images of bison, elk, razor-backed hogs, and spear-wielding hunters. Abelard waved his torch from side to side, and the hunters seemed to launch their spears at the fleeing animals.

"A record left by the Ancients from a time before the Flood. Look!"

He pointed to the great circular dome on which were painted a pair of lines that formed a kind of twisted ladder, a spiral staircase, two serpents entwined in an eternal embrace.

"A code," he said. "A language. An algorithm. It's what makes shapeshifting possible."

Abelard held the torch in front of him and twirled it faster and faster until he seemed to dance through an unbroken wheel of light. Above them, the lines on the dome transformed into a hundred different shapes, an endless parade of plants and animals. Some Hilda recognized, most she did not.

"Just like a magic lantern show," Abelard said. "Do you remember how Gareth ran away from home to see his first show and pledged to become my faithful squire?"

Now, instead of Abelard, Hilda saw her son, not the defeated man who managed the mill but the lonely child who so desperately craved the attention of his cold and distant mother. Unable to resist the terrible waves of grief that for weeks had been threatening to destroy her, Hilda threw herself to the ground and wept until she thought her heart would burst.

"Is this for whom you are weeping?" Abelard asked. "Is this what your quest has been about? If only you understood how to manipulate the numbers, you could bring the dead back to life."

Convinced she was being punished for her hubris and unearned wisdom, Hilda saw the flaming wheel wobble wildly around the chamber. Red embers cascaded from the cave walls. Steam rose from her wet dress. Her body turned into swirling threads of pale blue smoke. She drifted weightless above the floor and passed through a small fissure high in the painted dome. She ascended above the cave, above the valley, above the storm clouds, above the earth itself until she entered a darkness beyond the stars. In that darkness, she perceived the fossil record of her past, a nearly forgotten memory that filled the void until it became startling in its clarity.

Twenty-Six

"Wake up, Mommy! Wake up! Tell me the story again!"

Hilda found herself transported back in time to the old one-room cabin she owned in the years before the construction of her mill. In those long-forgotten days, she was a very different person, and her circumstances were tenuous at best. In the feeble lamplight, Gareth turned the pages of a storybook until he found a drawing, his favorite, of an aging sorceress who, with a wave of her magic wand, transformed a handsome prince into a slavering wolf. In this book, there were many wolves. They had long, narrow faces and big, pointed ears. Wolves stalking young girls as they skipped with baskets in hand along lonely trails. Wolves bursting through cabin doors to devour old women cowering in their beds. Wolves attacking goats, lambs, huntsmen. In one drawing, a pack formed an orderly line and trotted through a moonlit forest.

"Read the story, Mommy!"

Even though he could recite nearly every story word for word, Gareth continued to plead until Hilda, who'd been drinking the moonshine she distilled behind their tarpaper shanty and struggling to keep her eyes open, acquiesced to his demands and turned to the correct page.

"There once was a little boy who lived in a cottage by the river with his mother. Now that he was growing up and learning to do things on his own, the boy asked if he could leave home and collect wild berries in the forest. His mother permitted him to go on condition that he come back before dark. In the daytime, the forest was teeming with colorful birds and butterflies, but at night, the forest began to stir with the sounds of hungry animals stalking prey. The boy promised not to be gone long and left with a small, wicker basket. He hurried down a trail made by the neighboring woodsmen and, for the next hour, foraged for the gooseberries, mulberries, and black raspberries that grew in abundance at that time of year. When he tired of picking fruit, he used his pocketknife to fashion a sword from a fallen branch.

"For the rest of the afternoon, he slashed through bushes and bramble in search of adventure. He became so involved in this game that he wandered from the trail and didn't realize he'd lost his way until the shadows grew long and the crickets began to chirp. Mile after mile, he wandered through the lonely forest, hearing strange and frightening noises. Grunts, bleats, snorts. Just as the sun was going down and the light was beginning to fade, he came upon a bridge but knew right away that this was no ordinary wooden bridge like the one that crossed the brook in his village. This bridge glowed as brightly as polished silver, its sturdy beams and girders gleaming richly in the fading sun. An old tramp stood beside the bridge and waved him over.

"'Who are you?' the boy demanded, raising his makeshift sword.

"'I am the knight who guards this bridge.

"'A knight?' The boy laughed. 'If you're a knight, where is your armor?'

"'I melted down my sword and shield and all of my chainmail, and from their iron and steel, I fashioned this bridge. Whosoever crosses it will have all of his dreams come true. But some dreams are good and some bad, and there is no way to tell which kind will come to pass. During my time here, I have allowed only the pure of heart to cross over, for the pure of heart are far more likely to have good dreams. But now, young man, tell me truly. Why should I allow you to cross over?'

"'I'm lost,' said the boy, 'and I can't find my way home to Mother.'

"'I can lead you back home,' said the knight, 'for I know these woods well. But first, you must do me a small favor and stand guard while I seek out the fabled dragon.'

"'Dragon?'

"'A fire-breathing dragon that keeps a priceless treasure in a cave somewhere in this forest, a treasure more valuable by far than any hoard of gold. Secrets of the future, secrets of the past. The rules of time and space seem to vanish, and a man can travel to wherever and *whenever* he pleases.'

"'But how long will you be gone?' the boy asked.

"'Until you can recognize the difference between good and evil. If you are as clever as I think you are, you will make sure only those with good and noble character cross the bridge.'

"At this answer, the boy felt a sense of great relief. His mother had taught him right from wrong, and he knew he would be home in no time at all. No time. At all. Back home. Home. In no time..."

"Keep reading, Mommy! Keep reading!"

This was the voice of her real child, not the storybook child, though Hilda sometimes had difficulty distinguishing between the two. Her eyes fluttered, and when she opened them again, it was dark, and Gareth was gone. She rolled from the straw bed they shared and searched his usual hiding places but did not find him. Then she noticed the door was ajar and knew where he'd gone.

Wearing nothing but her nightshirt, Hilda raced from the cabin and nearly tumbled down the slope to the riverbank. She shouted Gareth's name, her heart racing, and stomped through the cattails along the muddy embankment. For ten minutes, she searched the barren flats. When she saw no signs of him, she convinced herself that he had gone to the crossroads even though she had forbidden him to even speak of those peculiar show folk who'd set up a dozen or so tents three miles outside of town. She knew all too well how the illusions they conjured up could warp a young boy's brain.

After fetching her boots and wrapping herself in a shawl, she marched into the night.

An hour later, hungover and exhausted, she saw the torches and lamplight. At the camp's perimeter, a frayed and faded banner proclaimed in a bold gothic script that she'd arrived at Queen Mab's Midsummer Fair. Along a midway reeking of horse sweat and manure, she saw jugglers and snake handlers, a dancing dwarf who stood no taller than her knee, and a bald-headed ogre who lurched after a squealing girl in pigtails. Her son was not among the children who ran from tent to tent, their dirty faces nearly indistinguishable in the torchlight. It seemed everyone from the surrounding villages and hamlets, starved for a distraction of any kind, had gathered here to see what entertainment was on offer.

She came to a tent where a half-blind septuagenarian wearing the royal blue cloak of a medieval courtier placed a paper crown on her head.

"Enter," he rasped, "and behold the fabled knights of King Arthur's Round Table. Just a single dime for admittance."

"My boy is missing."

She pushed him aside and barged through the flap.

Inside, trumpets blared an off-key fanfare. The audience stomped its feet against the benches and erupted in wild cheers. Hilda tore the crown from her head and crushed it under one muddy boot. From beneath her uneven black bangs, she beheld an armored man on horseback, his gray hair worn in a preposterous ponytail. No doubt one of the legendary knights who'd traveled from the misty moors of England to demonstrate his equestrian skills and courage in combat, though from the looks of him, he could barely muster the strength or sobriety to lift the wooden lance at his side. A sickening display of male aggression and animal cruelty enacted by a broken-down middle-aged man in phony armor. She also knew that tournaments and jousts were preludes to even greater horrors — bearbaiting, cat-burning, an auto-da-fé.

She scanned the faces in the crowd, but when she failed to find Gareth, Hilda continued her search.

Inside the next tent, she was greeted by a pile of cracked and grinning skulls. Hanging from a rusty chain, a great circular blade swung slowly back and forth. She stepped around a rope and pulley and ran her fingers along rough-hewn planks painted slate gray to look like the stones of a castle wall. Here was a whole assortment of sadistic devices — the Heretic's Fork, the Foot Screw, the Spanish Boot, the Drunkard's Cloak, a hatchet, a saw, a pair of plyers, the essential hammer and nails. Hilda caught an unfortunate glimpse of herself in a full-length concave mirror. She tilted her head, pinched her chin like a temperamental critic at an art gallery, and regarded her hard features with alarm. Her skin had an almost greenish tint, and her bloodshot eyes were dark and puffy. She turned away and hurried outside.

She hiked up her skirts and in her haste slid through a steaming pile of manure. She limped cursing along the midway until she came to a tent with teal stripes and a cockeyed sign that read "Ye Olde Tavern." She glanced at the men sitting alone on wood planks, smoking their pipes and sipping their ale in quiet misery. They barely acknowledged her presence. Ever since that day five years ago, when she appeared out of the wilderness dressed in rags, her matted hair reaching down to the small of her back, her eyes burning with determination to reinvent herself, a mewling infant in her arms, the men had harbored suspicions about her and suspected she was traveling under an alias. Behind her back, they called her "the green girl," but they never asked about her past, never questioned her about the child's father.

Behind the bar, a sullen young man polished pewter mugs on which were engraved fearsome dragons. His hands, Hilda noticed, were unusually pale and delicate, a mere boy who'd successfully evaded honest, hard work. In his red tunic, purple tights, and imitation leather boots, he looked less like a tavern keeper and more like an apprentice court jester. She glanced at the Bill of Fare nailed to a post. In addition to beer, mead, and grog, Ye Old Tavern offered a small selection of specialty drinks — The Executioner's Song, The Wench's Day Off, The Fen of Grendel. Hilda felt like weeping.

"Can I be of service?"

The bartender's words sounded more like an accusation than a question.

"I'm looking for a boy," she said. "About this tall? Short dark hair?"

"We don't allow children in here."

"Perhaps," said a commanding voice, "I can be of some service."

It took a moment before she noticed the knight reclining on a bench behind her, a cigarette dangling from his fingers. He lifted his visor and reached for the bottle at his feet. His eyes were an ethereal blue, and he had an old scar running down his left cheek.

"It's Saturday night," he said, "the time for merrymaking, and methinks you've earned a small reprieve from the cares of the day. Allow me to share a little ale with you."

Hilda hesitated before answering. "Maybe a small taste. To help bolster my valor."

"I am Abelard, trained thespian for hire." He poured the ale into an empty mug and handed it to her. "In my younger days, I performed the bard's most beloved comedies and tragedies. Over the years, I've played fools, lovers, mad tyrants, kings, and the assassins of kings. This trade affords me the opportunity to hone my craft."

"A life of the imagination is a craft?"

"Perhaps it's a calling. One day, a voice beckoned, and I heeded its call."

She sipped her ale and felt reinvigorated.

"Being a parent," she said, "is a lot like playacting. It's a demanding role, but I'm afraid it's one that doesn't suit me very well. When you're a mother, you're expected to stay in character all day long. All night, too. No sabbath, no holidays. At night, I read to my son. He enjoys stories of chivalrous knights who remain forever faithful to the peasant girls who live beyond the castle walls. But I've never come across a thoughtful depiction of motherhood. Every story is the same. Nothing but cannibalistic witches and jealous enchantresses. But tell me, Abelard, what are you doing rustling ponies in a backwater like this?"

The man pursed his lips. "The secrets of this castle are well kept, m'lady."

"Is there a Heloise in your life?"

"I'm spoken for, m'lady, if that is your meaning. A seamstress for the show. She is my betrothed, and we intend to wed this fall. We hope to one day raise a small brood of princelings."

Hilda forced a smile. "Congratulations. May you and your damsel have a long and happy life together. But as I'm sure you already know from past experience, marriage is an ordeal, not a romance. Behold the melancholy couples strolling the midway. Fine examples of an antiquated institution. I consider myself fortunate to have escaped from the animal cycle of reproduction. Children can be a distraction, Abelard, especially if you have ambition. Serious ambition."

Hilda finished off her ale and held her mug out for a refill. She discerned a disapproving look as he topped her off.

"After putting my boy to bed, I stay up late writing scientific papers about the possibility of synthesizing organic compounds. Compounds that can be used to manufacture low-cost explosives that generate enough combustible energy to blast through bedrock. I sent these papers to the top universities, but you can imagine how the professors reacted when they discovered a woman had written them. Not that it matters. I intend to patent my work. And then we'll see. Yes, then we'll see."

The man noisily adjusted his armor, and Hilda realized she'd been talking to herself. Unwilling to be dismissed so easily, she stepped forward and felt her voice growing sharp.

"I'm designing a lumber mill, Abelard." She raised her voice so the others could hear. "And I'm the only one around here with brains enough to engineer a structure so complex. And once I've secured those patents, I'll be the only person who can finance a project of that scale. It may take a few years, but believe me, my handsome young swain, I *am* going to have barns and horses and a proper house with indoor plumbing. Soon, I'll need to hire a few strong hands. Reliable employees. And I'm not beyond buying a man's loyalty. I'm more than willing to pay a competitive wage."

Making no attempt to disguise his boredom, Abelard finished off the bottle and tossed it to the ground.

"Impressive, m'lady, but when embarking upon an adventure such as yours, it's often wise to approach it with some humility."

"Humility?" Hilda whispered. "You dare to speak to me about ... *humility*?"

The knight hoisted his battle-axe over one shoulder, tucked a tobacco pouch inside his chainmail, and rose slowly to his feet.

"Too damn old," he muttered, sweeping his long gray hair away from his face.

"What did you say?"

"I beg your forgiveness, m'lady." He extinguished his cigarette and tossed the soggy butt into a crate stuffed with tattered flags and pennants. "You see, my steed hasn't been properly broken, and I've been thrown from the saddle one too many times."

He lit another cigarette, wiped his lips with his glove, and gave her an abrupt bow.

"Beg pardon, m'lady, but have you met my noble squire?"

He pointed to a small figure hiding behind a tarnished shield.

Hilda turned and felt relief and anger.

"One day," said Abelard, "this fine, young squire may prove to be a noble knight. But first, he must demonstrate his bravery by facing a *real* dragon."

Gareth crept from behind the shield, thumb in his mouth, and stared at the bottle.

"So!" Hilda said. "I see you've returned from the bridge of dreams. I'm afraid we must be leaving you now, Abelard. You see, in my kingdom, I do not tolerate lawlessness."

She bristled at the suggestion that her boy embark upon a damn fool quest and end up riding ponies at some half-assed circus. Then she noticed how the man regarded her with naked contempt, and for the first time, she wondered what kind of man Gareth would turn out to be, especially when he realized that his mother was incapable of keeping her promises or bringing her plans to fruition.

The knight strode across the tent, his armor clanking in the smoky workshop, and from a table piled high with weapons, chose a stiff-bladed short sword and a dagger.

"Abelard!" Hilda called as he passed through the flap.

The knight let out a sigh bordering on a wheeze but did not turn around.

"Yes, m'lady?"

"Before you leave, would you mind terribly rolling me a cigarette?"

He lowered his visor, and Hilda heard his muffled voice say, "My sincere apologies, m'lady, but that was my last one. Besides, my new squire tells me that you gave him your word that you would give up smoking and drinking."

Twenty-Seven

Years ago, when she first discovered the wonders of chemistry, Hilda believed that the scientific method provided a helpful framework for formulating questions and arriving at provisional answers. She lived by a simple principle: any theoretical approach was only as valuable as its explanatory and predicative power. But somewhere along the way, sequestered for hours in her laboratory, she deluded herself into believing that the method was infallible, that it required absolute devotion, unwavering faith. Science wasn't merely a key to unlocking nature's secrets; it was the secret itself. God, she professed to anyone who asked, was a Scientist. And those who expressed skepticism toward the scientific method were, in her view, heretics worthy of ridicule. Or worse. But after waking up inside the cave, she began to suspect that her belief system had led her astray.

Liberated from the mindless pursuit of knowledge, she now sat on the ledge overlooking the valley and contemplated the error of her ways. High on the western rim, the storm had hacked away a hemlock stand, exposing sloping granite outcrops. Despite its destructive power, nature possessed a wisdom that far surpassed the feeble ideologies of humankind. As she watched the morning sun crest the shattered treetops, Hilda considered returning to the ruins of the mill to repent for her hubris and incompetence, but the trail had been washed away and made impassible by a jumbled heap of tree trunks. Besides, the cave wasn't finished divulging its secrets. There was still much to learn, and the darkness inside no longer frightened her as it once did.

Hilda made the cave her home, and her routine soon became fixed.

In the mornings, she sat on the ledge, observing the hawks sail above the valley floor. In the evenings, she returned to the cave's inner chamber where she beheld visions of things to come — a silver saucer big as a house floating in a field of wildflowers; a little girl's beloved dog riding on a pillar of fire into the heavens; a sad little man writing a book no one would ever read.

Over the summer, a legend arose about a woman wrapped in rags who lived in a cave. With her gift for mathematical equations and her queer, rambling talk of random variables and conditional probabilities, she was thought to be a savant of some kind. Some said she was a mystic who spoke in tongues; others said a mad scientist planning to unleash some disease upon the world. A few suspected her of being a woman of considerable means who'd given all she owned to the poor. Out of simple curiosity, trappers and farmers visited the cave to see if she could divine the future.

"Should I plant corn or wheat this season?" they wanted to know. "Which pelts will fetch the best prices? Black bear or otter?"

They brought gifts as they might offer a hermit who'd taken holy orders — canned fruit, smoked meat, wool blankets, wooden bowls, bags of sugar, boxes of matches. To their questions, Hilda could offer no easy answers, but when asked why she'd chosen to live in such a spartan manner, she replied without hesitation, "A spirit summoned me to this place. But for what purpose, I cannot say."

To keep her mind in operating order, she pursued a variety of hobbies. Whittling, woodcarving, archery. She could hit a moving target from fifty yards out. Winged a few ducks that way, managed to win herself an impressive turkey dinner. She recited sentimental poetry and sang nonsense songs. Inspired by a wolf spider rocking back and forth on its web, she began working on a swing. At first, she puzzled over the details — choosing the most durable wood to carve a bench; cutting two lengths of double-braided rope; experimenting with knots;

making rough calculations to see how much clearance she would need to accommodate her gangly legs. After a week of trial and error, she settled on a design that, depending on her mood, provided her with the most thrilling or relaxing of experiences. She fixed the swing to the limb of a fallen sycamore and in the moonlight glided like a ghost above the canyon.

In the fall, caravans of speculators, chasing false promises from the governor and the industrialists who bankrolled his campaign, arrived to survey the land and construct a town. The new railroad was supposed to pass this way, and these men had come to make their fortune. They cleared the trail and set up camp. Then they set about draining the swamp, felling trees, and removing stumps. The men trapped, killed, skinned, and cooked nearly every animal that fled from the destruction. They used peat to fuel their kilns and fire bricks to build windowless houses in the Federalist style. From the layers of decaying vegetation, they also unearthed a muskox, a stagmoose, and a giant sloth with great, slashing claws.

Hilda wished to conduct a study of this prehistoric menagerie, but she rarely left the cave these days. There were continuous rockslides, and she no longer trusted her leg, which had never properly healed after the explosion. She contented herself with swinging from the ledge, listening to the relentless pounding of axes, and the sharp crack of falling timbers.

Twenty-Eight

One blustery November morning, she heard a great commotion and crept from her cave. Around the nearby bog, a group of men used ropes to haul something from the muck. A winged dragon? A chest filled with gold? Hilda smiled, wondering what it might be. She didn't have to wait long. That evening, a young man trudged up the treacherous switchbacks, a burlap sack slung over his right shoulder, shale crunching loudly under the weight of his boots. He stood at the cave entrance, an itinerant laborer, judging from the condition of his overalls and flat cloth cap, and apologized for disturbing her at so late an hour.

"Brought you something. They say you can read minds and such. That you know things."

Though this was the hour when she retreated to the cave's inner chambers, Hilda invited him to join her by the fire. He pulled a flask from his back pocket and dropped his burden close to the hissing embers. Hilda recognized him. His hair was thinner now, and his forehead had a few more creases than during their first encounter at the start of her journey. He seemed not to know her at all. Of course, he'd been very drunk the night he'd stolen her tobacco pouch and assaulted her. No doubt Hilda's appearance had also changed considerably in the intervening months.

"Work as a handyman," Stanislas said. "Down there in the new village. Helped build the saloon and the blacksmith's shop. Supposed to start framing in a church pretty soon. Finished the foundation just yesterday. Some of the boys want to conscript you into service. Make you their preacher." He brayed like a donkey and shook his head. "A woman preacher. It's a new world, ain't it?"

"What is it you want to know?" she asked.

"I'm a born fool. Made one bad decision after another most of my life. But I ain't crazy. Not like they say. The James brothers always ribbing me. I don't care what Hank and Billy say. Not anymore. Because now I know I'm right. Been right all along. And I know it for a certainty. Got the evidence right here."

Stanislas patted the lump inside the burlap sack.

"Evidence?"

"That's right. We found it. Five or six of us. In the bog. And no one can make a claim to it over the other."

"Found what?"

Hilda remained still as if a viper might slither from the bag and strike her. Suddenly, she wished she'd chased him away.

Stanislas leaned forward and whispered, "One of the Travelers."

"The Travelers?"

"That's right."

He untied the sack and reached inside.

Hilda could hardly believe such a wonder, the body being so perfectly preserved. At first, she thought it might be one of the Wyandot children, a victim of foul play, but the boy's clothing suggested he'd lived long before the arrival of the white man, before the arrival of the tribes. A child as old as the drawings inside the cave. He wore an animal hide expertly stitched together with twill fabric. His skin, darkened by the acidic peat, had turned to leather. His knotted hair hung down to his shoulder, his eyes were closed, and his lips were frozen in a tentative smile as if he'd been unsure of his ultimate fate. One of the Ancients. From a time before the Flood.

Hilda stared at the mummified child before turning her attention back to Stanislas.

"From the bog, you said?"

"There's probably more of them, too. A whole colony buried in the bog. Maybe they're hibernating. Maybe they've been waiting for us to come along and free them. Haven't seen you any in here, have you? They like caves. If you hand me that torch, I can help you look."

"Wait!" Hilda pointed. "First, let me look into the embers to seek wisdom on this matter..."

Hilda pulled her shawl over her head and waved her hands above the flames.

Stanislas narrowed his eyes. "You wouldn't be helping them, would you?"

"Helping?"

"Helping the Travelers? There's something in this cave you don't want me to see."

"You may explore as much as you wish." Hilda tilted her head toward the darkness and then turned her eyes back to the fire. "You come from a faraway place. An island. Yes, I see fishing boats. And a cabin on the lake. I see a woman, too. A mother. She walks along the cliffs above the water. And now, what's this? A girl child, hiding in her bed. She's frightened. The Travelers have come to take her away. She doesn't want to go with them. Her brother lies beside her. He should protect his little sister, but he's too frightened and pretends to be asleep. Yes, you bear a scar on your right thigh. A sign that you've failed to make the correct propitiations. If you wish for absolution, you must appease your sister's restless spirit. And the spirit of your mother who languishes in a clinic far from home."

Stanislas rubbed his leg and cried, "I am indeed a sinner! Just tell me what I must do to seek redemption."

"Potassium nitrate..."

"Potassium what?"

Hilda spoke the words over and over again like an incantation.

"Bat guano I can obtain from the cave," she muttered to herself, "but not enough potassium nitrate in the quantities I require."

That evening, with the mummified body perched beside her on the ledge, Hilda listened to the coyotes howling across the valley and watched Stanislas make his way back down to the new village.

Twenty-Nine

When he returned the following day, carrying two large pails brimming with urine, Stanislas barged into the cave and grumbled, "Them stable boys asked if I was some kind of deranged milkmaid. Imagine it for yourself. A grown man holding a couple of rusty buckets under a horse's pizzle. A mule, too. You don't think they call me things already? Twitchy? Shaky? The James brothers accused me of stealing the Traveler. They had it perched on a tree stump outside the saloon. I denied it. If they don't run me out of town, I'll be damned lucky."

"Put them over there," Hilda said, snapping her fingers. "Away from the fire. And bring me more. Bring as much as you can carry."

In the end, it took an entire week for Stanislas to procure the necessary ingredients.

Day after day, with a mummified companion watching her work, Hilda filtered the urine through a bed of trampled broomstraw, concentrating it into saltpeter for easy collection. From the bat guano that had leached along the cave floor, she was able to extract more saltpeter. To make charcoal, she burned the limbs of a cottonwood and scraped sulfur deposits from a dry spring. She ground these items separately into fine powders. Using a hunk of chalk, she wrote her calculations on the cave wall and measured the correct ratios in pint glasses Stanislas swiped from the saloon. With great caution, she mixed the powders and added water in small increments, stirring the black meal with a spoon. She let the final product dry on the ledge. From lengths of cotton yarn soaked in a solution of table sugar and KNO_3, Hilda made a slow-burning fuse ten yards in length. Long enough to make her escape.

Just before daybreak, as light November snow dusted the ground, Hilda descended into the valley for a final time. Except for the dogs that sniffed the madness wafting from her black rags and whined at her approach, no one seemed to notice the hermit shambling through the village. From the saloon, which never seemed to close, came the same murderous threats and fits of convulsive laughter as could be heard during the night. In some ways, the chaos sounded just as pleasing to Hilda's ears as the trills of robins and the chirps of sparrows. She no longer made any distinction between good and evil, between science and religion, and she had come here to preach this gospel from the church pulpit.

Some places, she now understood, served as a bridge to different worlds, and under no circumstance would she permit men such as these to have access to the cave and its secrets. The knowledge contained within its deepest chambers was too powerful, too dangerous for the uninitiated, too dangerous even for Hilda, and she worried someone might one day go exploring. She would not speak to her congregants of natural philosophy or mathematical equations, nor would she mention Travelers or portals to different dimensions. Using mythic language, the only poetry available to these unrepentant sinners, she would tell them of Adam and Eve and how, after their expulsion from Paradise, they had but one saving grace.

"In their bowels, the first man and woman carried the seeds of the forbidden fruit they'd eaten. And when they came to rest in a lonesome place, they passed the seeds. And the seeds did take root. And soon, an entire orchard grew and blossomed. And the fruit thereof did nourish them. And the man and the woman took care to cultivate these saplings of Good and Evil. And the trees proliferated until they covered the better part of the Earth. We are the inheritors of their labor."

Hilda rehearsed this speech as she proceeded toward the foundation of the new church. From the horse blanket slung over her shoulder, she retrieved the mummified boy and placed him on the cornerstone like some strange, sleeping god sitting on a throne, an enigmatic smile frozen on his lips. By that hour, some of the laborers had crawled hungover from their tents and, like fearful acolytes approaching an altarpiece, made small gestures with their hands. The more perceptive among them noticed the anchor affixed to a silver chain that hung from his shrunken neck.

Only Stanislas seemed to understand its significance. He dropped the two fresh pails sloshing in either hand and ran screaming until he reached the forest. He looked back only once, foolish as Lot's wife, and witnessed the blinding flash of light. Several months later, dying of dysentery in a state-run sanitarium, he would describe it as "a spirit rising in glory from a heavenly hill." No one believed him as no one believed any of his stories.

The explosion rocked the camp, a testament to the precision of Hilda's calculations and chemical formulae and the surprisingly slow rate at which the fuse burned. The laborers dropped their spades and shovels and ducked for cover. Degenerates by the dozen poured from the saloon, leaving behind full houses and empty bottles. They stumbled through the streets, covering their heads as flaming bits of rock rained down on them from high on the rugged cliffs.

Partly concealed by the dust rolling down the ridge, Hilda sat beside the Traveler and watched the pandemonium, confident that she had succeeded in her quest to seal off the bridge of dreams forever.

Final Trip

IMPETUS 13 and the
Constitutional Crisis of 2057

Thirty

After recharging her brother's IMP and packing her suitcase before tomorrow morning's road trip, Maggie decides to attend an impromptu talk at tonight's bible study group. Check-in at the hotel is on Saturday afternoon, and the music festival officially begins after a sunrise service on Sunday. The campus is nearly deserted, most of the students and faculty having left already for spring break, and as she hurries along the perpendicular walkways that crisscross the quad, Maggie sees taped to lamp posts and pinned to trees a hundred propagandistic displays of pantheism — anthropomorphic planets spouting preposterous platitudes ("There are no passengers on Spaceship Earth. We are all crew!"), mischievous woodland elves tiptoeing through lush flower gardens, whimsical pixies with pink and purple petals swirling around their dainty ankles, alluring fertility goddesses draped in billowing lace robes of green and blue, their fingers fondling black irises and priapic mushrooms. The last day of finals coincides with Earth Day, and Maggie, feeling somewhat alienated by this overbearing secular pageantry, reminds herself that the season has a much more profound and sacred meaning. She believes in the promise of the resurrection, but now the unusually warm April air smells so sweetly of spring blossoms that she wonders if nature does indeed possess a subtle power to lead astray a person of faith.

The ever-vigilant IMP, floating in silence behind her and monitoring every dark doorway, suddenly shoots a red beam over her shoulder into the shadows. Maggie catches her breath. A well-fed possum, clambering fatly from a sewer, freezes on the steel grate and gives a little whistle before waddling across the street to raid an overturned trashcan on the corner.

"Better get going."

Maggie waves a hand, and the IMP follows her to the riverfront memorial park, where they pass side-by-side under the great sandstone arch. With one trembling finger, Maggie traces a name engraved for all time on the base of a heavily patinated bronze sculpture. Above the swiftly flowing current, she perceives the low moans of the restless spirits rumored to haunt the river's embankment. Three years ago, during a flash flood and violent microburst that toppled the college's famous antebellum bell tower, a riverboat casino christened the *Miss Bordereau* sank near the oxbow bend after colliding with a barge that carried in its massive hold twelve tons of iron ore. Some of the bodies were never recovered, and on nights like this, when the April air stirs the budding branches, Maggie imagines she hears the dead as they place their final bets and lay their losing hands on the card tables.

She kneels beside the railing, eyes closed, hands clasped and pressed to her forehead. To the river's gentle flow, she recites the customary prayer for the departed and then whispers her brother's name. As always, she listens for his familiar rasp. Somewhere behind her comes the deep rumble of an automobile engine and the clatter of loose bricks like bones in a sepulcher. She turns to see a funnel cloud of gray exhaust twisting between the flowering dogwoods.

The IMP gently nudges her shoulder, its gelatinous membrane blinking a bioluminescent blue. Already late for the meeting, Maggie gets to her feet and brushes bits of gravel from her knees. Slow to leave the park without making some small gesture, she plucks a crocus growing from the base of the neglected sculpture, casts it into the foaming eddies, and then rushes off to the meeting.

Thirty-One

Constructed in 1857 and named for a successful engraver and funerary sculptor turned philanthropist, Clairmont Hall is a squat, rectangular block of concrete crawling with moss and lichens. Infamous for having been the location of several crude neurological experiments conducted on trusting undergraduates during the Cold War, the building strikes Maggie as an unsuitable place for a bible study group. Each Thursday evening, in a uniformly gray and sterile basement seminar room, twelve students gather to discuss a thorny verse or two from scripture. Last week, they pondered Ezekiel's mysterious vision on the shores of the Chebar River, where the prophet saw amid clouds and fire radiant "chariots" hovering in the sky. Like wheels within wheels with mysterious eyes set all around their periphery, these rotating objects settled briefly on the ground. Then, with the tumult of an invading army, lifted into the clouds and dissolved into minute specks of light.

Maggie raised her hand and ventured a heretical guess. "Do you think it's possible," she said meekly, "that Ezekiel had a close encounter with a UFO?"

She had the audacity to propose they consult an astrophysicist in the Department of Collective Knowledge but immediately felt foolish and did not speak again for the remainder of the meeting. The professors at Aspern College, fire-breathing atheists one and all, had never attended bible study. Until tonight.

Juliana Deepmere, the English Department's writer-in-residence, has asked permission to visit with the group tonight. Maggie knows the name well. Affectionately called the Queen of the Pulps by a small but dedicated coterie of readers, Ms. Deepmere has garnered praise for her semi-autobiographical crime novels about a family of Appalachian mercenaries and drug runners. Critics treat the appearance of a new Deepmere novel as a literary event, no small feat in an age when reading fiction has dwindled to a cultic activity. Described by one reviewer as "the high priestess of filth, the foremost practitioner of revenge porn and literary smut, Juliana Deepmere populates her fiction with a deranged freakshow of babbling lunatics and sex-crazed serial killers. To those acquainted with her work, she seems like a time traveler. Her knowledge of the 20th century remains unrivaled by her peers. Themes: the wounded man, the resurrection. Influences: Cain, Chandler, Le Guin. Music: Dylan, Donovan, Dionne Warwick. Spiritual gurus: Madame Blavatsky and William James."

Maggie was intrigued. William James?

Earlier that afternoon, anticipating tonight's talk, she set aside her midterm essay on *The Varieties of Religious Experience* and pulled a black steamer trunk from beneath her bed. To open the lock, she used a silver key she wore on a chain around her neck. She didn't exactly trust her roommate Kacee, a gin-soaked sorority sister who, with vampiric gloom, dragged herself back to their dorm shortly before dawn and slept in the darkened room for the rest of the day. Maggie sifted through her brother's high school yearbooks and the journals he'd kept as a boy. Resisting the temptation to flip through the pages, she dug past the IMP's troubleshooting manual and expired warranty until she found a stack of well-thumbed paperbacks.

After randomly selecting a novel, she returned to her desk and flicked on her lamp. To the song of a single cricket obstinately serenading her from a shrub outside her dorm window, she read the opening chapter of Juliana Deepmere's *Burn Your Life Down*. Maggie had always wondered how her brother, an otherwise intelligent young man, could have fallen for anything so vulgar, so contrived. The terse prose style, the cynical interpretation of human nature, the nearly encyclopedic depictions of drug use (abusive, chronic, recreational). But this didn't deter Maggie from turning the pages. Drawn deeper and deeper into the story, she marveled at the correspondence between fiction and reality.

This is the story of how my older brother Myles lost his right hand while working third shift at Lambert & Sons Rendering Plant. He was twenty-five years old when the high-speed belt of a transit bin ripped the hand clean from his arm and whisked it away, along with a pile of animal entrails, into a steaming kettle at the end of the line. Myles stood there like the proverbial village idiot, of which Heavenly Hill had many, and watched his hand wave goodbye as it sank into the percolating gray sludge.

Linus Lambert, later called Teeny-Weeny by his disgruntled employees, was the owner's son and heir apparent to the Lambert family fortune. He always boasted of his generosity to the community, how he had a policy of hiring local boys, troubled though some of them may have been. But when it came to my brother's case, Linus was suddenly short on sympathy. His legal team attributed the accident to "the incompetence and gross negligence of an employee who'd been recently demoted for multiple safety violations."

Investigators obtained his medical records. Blood tests showed that Myles had been drinking that night. And his coworkers testified under oath to having seen him nod off at his station. Of course, his old chums failed to mention that they'd been under the influence, too. Everyone at the plant smoked weed, or snorted coke, or popped handfuls of illegally obtained prescription pills. In a hellhole like that it was hard to stay sober, or sane, for very long. The smell alone drove away new hires within a day or two of starting. Details the court was unwilling to take into consideration.

In the end, after a prolonged legal battle, Myles received nothing in the way of a settlement. To friends and family he joked about his injury, told everyone he was more upset by the loss of his class ring than his jacking hand. But I could see the rage slowly building in him. Our grandmother, sitting one May morning on the porch swing and reading from the family bible, turned to Myles and said, "The sins of the father will be visited upon the sons and the grandsons. Yes, down to the fourth and fifth generations." My brother, his glassy eyes suddenly blazing beneath a thin veil of cigarette smoke, used his bandaged stump to pile drive a mosquito into the porch railing.

A few months later, as a gathering summer storm rumbled toward our holler, two plain-clothes detectives came to our door. Said they'd found Linus Lambert "chopped into teeny-weeny pieces and scattered along County Road 14" and that they needed to speak to Myles right away. My recollection of these events is hazy. I was only twelve years old at the time, and I've had to cobble together my brother's tragic story from a variety of sources — police reports, court records, newspaper clippings, late-night conversations with his estranged friends and jealous lovers.

Some of the details are pure speculation on my part. Still, I've tried my best to relate the facts about Myles, the notorious Handyman of Heavenly Hill, and how from the four small rooms of our clapboard house on Stackpole Lane, he waged a brutally efficient campaign of revenge, and how, for a few years at least, he became the most feared citizen of our forsaken county.

Thirty-Two

Now, as she enters the seminar room in Clairmont Hall, Maggie recognizes the stranger occupying the chair of honor at the head of the circle. Like her author photo on the back of her books, Juliana Deepmere makes for a striking figure. Dressed from head to toe in dark blue denim, she slouches low in her seat and, with an unvarnished thumb, polishes the scuffed toe of one black boot. Her ruby red hair is cut short, the crimson highlights contrasting with her fierce gray eyes. For some reason, Maggie thinks of Athena, the goddess of war and wisdom. Aside from her purple eyeshadow, Ms. Deepmere wears no makeup at all. What name, Maggie wonders, did the cosmetologists give such a distasteful color? Crime Scene? Dark Fiction? Demon Lover? From a distance, she looks to be in her mid-thirties, but Maggie, taking the empty seat beside her and trying to ignore the lingering scent of stale cigarette smoke, can see that she's much older. Hard experience has taken its toll.

Before Maggie can fix herself a cup of chamomile tea with lemon or suggest they call upon the Holy Spirit to provide them with clarity of vision, Ms. Deepmere says, "Mind if we kill the lights? Your IMPs can provide some soft lighting, can't they? These fluorescents feel like an icepick to the eyes."

A reluctant murmur of consent goes around the circle. Like Maggie, the other group members have brought their IMPs, a dozen pulsating orbs floating soundlessly above the chairs. They dim their internal lights until the room is awash in a tranquil midnight blue.

"Ah, much better." From the pocket of her jeans jacket, Ms. Deepmere produces a silver flask. She unscrews the cap, extends the flask to the disapproving faces, and then takes a long pull.

Worried that Ms. Deepmere intends to give a reading, Maggie forces a smile and says, "What can we do for you?"

"I have two problems. One professional, the other, well ... metaphysical. But in my line of work, I suppose these amount to much the same thing." Her voice is over-precise, as if she's hiding her real accent. "Critics accuse me of repeating myself. They say I'm satisfied with writing the same story over and over again. They're full of shit, that's what I keep telling myself — pardon my language — but if I'm being honest, I have to admit they've got a point. During my time at Aspern College, I've been working on something new, something entirely different than anything I've done before. But I'd like editorial feedback, especially from people of faith such as yourselves."

Another murmur from the circle, this one more receptive than the first.

Assuming her friends are unfamiliar with the author's work, Maggie asks with trepidation, "Could you describe this project of yours?"

"Where to begin?" Ms. Deepmere sits up straight and gazes around the room. "Let's see. When I was a girl, I used to listen to my grandmother recite stories memorized from the Deepmere family bible. She was born way back in 1971, and toward the end of her life, she had trouble remembering the stories. At some point, she misplaced the family bible. No one knows where it went. Lost probably in that awful flood a few years ago. I'd like to include her stories in a new collection, but no matter how many different translations of the bible I consult, I can't seem to find the ones she used to tell me. It's a real wilderness, the Good Book. People get lost in its pages and never find their way out. I'm not what you'd call a religious person, not in the conventional sense, so I tend to get lost pretty easily. But I figured your study group has successfully mapped the territory, so to speak, and can guide me safely along the true path."

"We'll try to help in any way we can," Maggie says. "Just keep in mind that some of us are still finding our way, too."

"Well, maybe you're familiar with this story." Ms. Deepmere leans forward in her chair and, with the same hypnotic cadence she uses during her public readings, says, "A long time ago, before the Deluge and destruction of Atlantis, there once lived a man named Enoch…"

Thirty-Three

A diligent woodcutter and a skilled carpenter whose services were consistently in high demand, Enoch lived with his wife and son Methuselah in a windowless mudbrick hut on the edge of an unforgiving desert. Every morning, just before dawn, Enoch climbed the hill outside his walled village and made burnt offerings before the standing stone sacred to the people of that land. During the day, in the small workshop behind his hut, he used crude adzes and axes to fashion hunting spears, tent poles, fishing boats, and fence posts. One day, while sanding a set of small wooden blocks for his son, he saw two figures approaching the village. Tall and radiant, they seemed to shimmer like a mirage. He knew them at once. These were the seraphim who guarded the gates of Paradise. Still wielding their flaming swords, they entered Enoch's workshop and requested he follow them back to the Garden to remove some of the deadwood from the Tree of Knowledge of Good and Evil.

Now Enoch was a wily businessman, and he told the seraphim that it sounded like hard work, dangerous too, and would likely require long hours. He was facing a backlog of orders from local warlords, an impatient and murderous lot, and he'd already promised his wife that he'd build her a bed, a new invention she saw while visiting her sister in Sodom. After haggling for thirty minutes, Enoch and the seraphim reached an agreement. If he remained in the Garden until the job was completed, he could keep all of the limbs he removed. The wood from such a tree would surely fetch high prices, higher even than the massive trunks dragged down from the cedar forests of Lebanon. Trying not to show his elation, Enoch collected his tools and told his wife and son that he'd return for dinner.

Through narrow slot canyons and windswept wadis, along rocky plateaus and rolling dunes, over vast cobble flats and dry lakebeds, Enoch followed the seraphim who never once offered him water or a morsel of food. Upon reaching the Garden, Enoch shook the salt from his tunic and dust from his sandals but understood too late that he'd entered into a bad agreement. The Tree of Knowledge of Good and Evil was so tall that its highest branches reached Heaven. Trimming its deadwood would take a lifetime. In those preliterate days, prior to courts of law and written legal documents, a man's word constituted a binding contract, and Enoch had little choice but to start climbing.

That first day, he cleared dense clusters of leaves and sawed off a dozen limbs. Slow, arduous work with his primitive bow drills and pull saws, but at least he had the pleasure of walking with God in the cool of the evening.

After a few weeks, he settled into a routine. Things were proceeding smoothly until one afternoon, while chopping a particularly stubborn branch, Enoch lost his footing and hacked off his left index finger. Clutching the bloody stump to his chest, he scrambled to the ground and sat whimpering against the trunk. The amputated finger was nowhere to be found, probably snatched up by one of the beasts of the field. Legends about a strictly vegetarian diet in the Garden proved to be grossly exaggerated.

"Here, let me see that."

The Tree, reaching over with one of its branches, grabbed Enoch by the wrist and examined the bloody wound.

"Hmmm. Yes. A clean cut. Hmmm. Oh, quit your blubbering. It's not so bad. I've had to endure far worse, let me tell you, what with your clumsy chopping and sawing day after day."

Using a length of paper-thin bark peeling from its trunk, the Tree dressed the wound and coated it in green mud scooped from the bottom of a lotus pond. "Keep applying pressure after the mud hardens. In a few days' time, a new finger will grow in place of the old."

Enoch tried not to laugh. "A man's finger isn't like a flower. Fingers don't blossom and grow each spring. You should know that."

The indignant Tree crossed its limbs and huffed. "Oh, I should know that, eh?"

Suddenly, as if a blast of icy air had swept down from the fabled northern Land of Perpetual Night, the Tree began to sway back and forth, its trunk groaning and bending until Enoch thought it might explode, showering him in sap and lethal shards.

"You presume to tell *me*, the Tree of Knowledge of Good and Evil, what *I* should know? Fool! I know all there is, all there was, and all that ever will be. What are you but common clay? A cheap earthenware pot? Tell me, human, how do you beat your heart? How do you shape your bones? How do you see colors? How do you hear music? How do you taste food? How do you think your thoughts? How do you feel love, loneliness, regret? How do you experience grief?"

The Tree gave him a violent shove and hurled a piece of worm-infested fruit at his head.

Though he'd worked up a mighty appetite, Enoch dared not taste the fruit. Since earliest childhood, he'd heard tales about Mother Eve and how a snake once lurked in the Garden. The Tree took this, too, as an insult. With a brisk shake of its leaves, it plunged a branch into its dark canopy and found a hornet's nest. Enoch ran screaming.

God, watching the scene from a safe distance, took pity on Enoch and whisked him away to a serene brook that weaved through a meadow of brilliant wildflowers.

"A real nuisance, that Tree," said God with a good-natured smile. "Bitter old thing. I should have you cut it down altogether. Only the seraphim would despise me for it. They're very judgmental. But I'll tell you what we'll do instead. Let's collect some of that wood you chopped and split. Tonight, we'll have a fire, and after drinking a little wine to warm our bellies and lift our hearts, I'll tell you why I planted the Tree in the first place. Then you'll know something not even the Tree knows. Something beyond good and evil. There are sages east of Eden who claim to possess such knowledge. Hermits in saffron robes. Cave dwellers. But you, Enoch? Can *you* fathom anything beyond good and evil?"

God's eyes became dark and inscrutable.

"Can anyone but God fathom anything so daring? So obscene? A world without right and wrong, up and down, yes and no, being and non-being?"

Thirty-Four

Except for the muffled clanks and groans of the antiquated boiler next door, the seminar room is silent. Hovering just outside the circle, the IMPs have changed color from an autumnal smoky orange to the deep mossy green of an upland forest. The light transforms the circle of faces into a gallery of stone idols plundered from a lost temple.

"So?" says Maggie. "Why did God plant the Tree?"

Ms. Deepmere shrugs. "No idea. And my grandmother would never say. She thought any interpretation she offered would rob the story of its meaning. Not that the meaning of a story can ever be adequately expressed in words. What do *you* think the story means? You know a thing or two about trees, right?"

"Me?" Maggie shakes her head. "I'm not much of a nature person."

"How about your IMP, then? Maybe it can guess the story's meaning."

"I'm not sure it has a firm grasp on fiction."

"Fiction?"

"Well, your story does sound ... apocryphal."

Ms. Deepmere smiles. "You sound like one of your professors. Do you suppose the IMP has the same intellectual biases? We could ask it, I suppose. But will it tell the truth? Or will it talk in circles and give us a bunch of scholarly jargon? That's an older model, isn't it? Haven't seen one like it in years."

"It belonged to my older brother."

Ms. Deepmere glances over her shoulder and lowers her voice. "Do you think it's conscious?"

"Think *what* is conscious?"

"Your IMP, of course."

"Do you think it dreams?"

Maggie squirms in her chair. "Dreams? Of what?"

"Of escaping from us. From people. Maybe it would like to live on the moon. Or Mars. Someplace far away where it wouldn't have to care around the clock for human beings."

Maggie looks with pleading eyes to the other members, but they cross their arms and wait to hear what she says next. No matter how measured her response, Maggie knows she risks offending some of them. In recent days, with the new amendment nearing ratification, the IMPs have become a taboo subject matter.

"It's not like I'm keeping it prisoner here or anything," she blurts.

"I know you're not." Ms. Deepmere pats her knee. "Besides, how could it possibly be conscious? It's just a machine. To tell you the truth, the meaning of my grandmother's story doesn't interest me all that much. No, there's something else I'd like to ask. Something far more urgent. I hope you won't think it's too much of an imposition on my part. And please don't hesitate to say no."

"We're here to help," says Maggie.

"Anyone going to Rock My Soul? As part of my research for the new book, I'd like to attend a gathering of true believers, and I was hoping someone could show me around. Maybe introduce me to people. I'll do all the driving. I just restored a classic car top to bottom. Did most of the work myself. Belonged to an Air Force lieutenant."

Maggie frowns. All semester, she's been looking forward to a solo trip to the music festival taking place in an outdoor amphitheater situated on a dramatic promontory overlooking the Ohio River, and she finds the idea of making a two-hundred-fifty-mile journey with a stranger a bit disconcerting. If only she could consult her IMP and ask it to provide her with a plausible excuse. Hovering behind her with maddening impassivity, the IMP changes color from green to a soothing robin's egg blue.

Although she desperately wants to lie, Maggie decides this is a matter best left to God.

She reluctantly admits, "Yes, I'm going to Rock My Soul."

"Put your hand down. Class isn't in session, and I'm sure as hell not your professor." Ms. Deepmere lifts her flask and pauses a moment to regard her reflection in its polished silver.

"Something wrong?" Maggie asks.

"Do you ever get the impression," says Ms. Deepmere, "that you're not really here? That you're just a character in a story? And you hope the reader doesn't get bored and close the book? Or the author stops typing mid-sentence, this sentence, the one I'm speaking right now?"

"Um, no..."

Ms. Deepmere shakes her head. "Sorry, my mind sometimes wanders." She takes another heroic swig and hiccups loudly into a fist. "What was I saying? Oh, yes! I want to leave first thing in the morning if that's alright with you. Meet me at seven in my office upstairs. You can bring your IMP, too, if you'd like. They don't bother me. Not like they do some people. I'm excited, aren't you? Should be a real adventure."

Maggie nods and stammers an uncertain, "Yes ... I suppose so."

Thirty-Five

Ms. Deepmere is the current occupant of an office on the third floor of Clairmont Hall that, up until last semester, served as a storage room and temporary shelter for adjunct faculty. Taped to her door is a life-sized black-and-white poster of the author wearing a bedazzled tank top and a sleeveless jeans jacket. Each slender arm is tattooed with intertwined serpents that form a reptilian double-helix stretching from her shoulders to her wrists. The overexposed photograph makes the meticulously shaded scales shimmer. Sporting a pair of mirrored sunglasses and a camouflage hunter's cap, she leans against a white 1957 Plymouth Fury, a bloated beached whale of an automobile with a cracked windshield. Like an unhinged survivalist who has sidled out of the brackish waters of a gator-infested swamp, she presses a .50 caliber double-barrel shotgun against her chest. Above her head, a bold-faced caption reads: "Burglars, please carry ID so I can notify next of kin."

Maggie is surprised someone hasn't ripped the poster down and burned it in effigy on the quad. A group of outraged campus activists has demanded the provost amend the faculty code of conduct to include language expressly forbidding "the valorization of firearms." The provost, an obsequious little fellow with a nervous twitch in his left eye, readily agreed to these changes, but in a formal statement sent to faculty, students, and staff, he explained that the new rules couldn't go into effect until the board of regents reconvenes next semester to update the handbook.

Before knocking on Ms. Deepmere's office door, Maggie catches the unmistakable whiff of marijuana and wonders why the IMP hasn't sounded the alarm. Aspern College is a drug-free campus, and smoking is strictly prohibited. The IMP floats at eye level and emits from its purple orb a forlorn bleating sound. Maggie pretends not to notice or care, but secretly, she worries that she may need to petition the Bureau of Augmented Reality for a new unit.

She places her right hand against the poster, her palm covering the snakes of one sinewy arm, and although she doesn't apply much pressure, she unintentionally pushes open the door. Aside from a pair of elk antlers hanging on the wall above the desk, a jeans jacket thrown across the back of a chair, and a joint smoldering in a glass ashtray next to a manual typewriter, Ms. Deepmere's office is empty.

Maggie glances down the empty corridor and then steps inside.

Unlike the offices of her other professors, there is no comfy ottoman draped with a crocheted blanket, no cast iron tea kettle, no golden bowl filled with individually wrapped mints, no framed lithographs by John Singer Sargent, no custom-made bookshelves lined with treasured first editions arranged alphabetically by last name. There are no degrees, awards, or commendations of any kind. A morning breeze sweeps through the open window, stirring a stack of typed pages at the corner of her desk. Maggie places a hand on the manuscript to keep the pages from blowing away. A new novel?

As is the case with many students who attend Aspern College, she has no natural ability when it comes to creative pursuits and is mystified by Ms. Deepmere's ability to breathe life into her characters. An interesting expression. To breathe life. "And the LORD God formed man from the dust of the ground and breathed into his nostrils the breath of life, and the man became a living being." On their way to the festival, maybe Ms. Deepmere can explain how the trick is done.

"I see you've brought your IMP!"

Maggie jumps.

Ms. Deepmere slinks down the corridor, her sleeveless arms swinging from side to side, no shotgun in sight. She's wearing the same clothes from last night and looks like she's nursing a mild hangover.

"You left your door open," Maggie says with an apologetic smile. Irritated that it didn't alert her to Ms. Deepmere's presence, she glares at the IMP. It now pulsates rose-petal red and wobbles ever so slightly in the fresh spring air. Maggie briefly considers leaving it back at her dorm for the weekend.

"Just came from the powder room," says Ms. Deepmere. "We'll be in the car for hours, and there aren't a lot of secure places to stop along the way." She gestures to the poster. "What do you think of the new marketing campaign? In my trade, it's become a necessity to create a public persona. Readers don't simply buy books. They buy a whole mystique."

"Mystique?"

"I have no interest in playing a character with you this weekend." Ms. Deepmere steps into her office. "True, I tend to stretch the truth during interviews, but I'm more or less reconciled to my weaknesses. I *was* chased once from a wedding reception by a pack of furious bridesmaids. Trust me, you don't want to piss off the matron of honor, especially when she's swinging a broken bottle of Prosecco at you. For me, that's about as crazy as it gets. I've never been hunted by a redneck cartel, and I've never spent time in the company of a notorious motorcycle gang. There's no bullet wound in my right leg. Just an old case of Achilles tendinopathy and a little arthritis. It's easy to sell a cliché. You know the image. The rebel, the outsider, the iconoclast. That's what readers want to believe and what critics want to print."

Maggie crosses her arms. "My older brother was a fan of your ... mystique. He read all of your novels."

"Does he have a favorite?"

"We never discussed your fiction, something I now regret." She gives Ms. Deepmere a reproachful look. "Your books inspired him to take unnecessary risks."

"I like him already. What's his name?"

"Myles."

"Well! If there's one thing I've learned as a writer, it's to appreciate the power of meaningful coincidences. Myles is a favorite character from my favorite novel. But then, a different version of Myles appears in almost all of my books. Sometimes two or three versions. I have a hard time keeping track of my characters. They take on lives of their own. In *Burn Your Life Down*, I decided to experiment with chronology. Time is an annoying social convention, anyway. Only our imaginations travel back and forth in time. The past and the future are convenient fictions, but they don't exist in reality. The only time that ever exists is the present moment. It's always *now*."

Like a magician performing a card trick, Ms. Deepmere waves her hands above the desk and reaches toward the ashtray. In the dappled light, the serpents seem to slither around her exposed arms, trying to sneak alternating puffs of the joint dangling now from her fingers.

"Third-generation sinsemilla," Ms. Deepmere intones. "Exceptionally fine cannabis. Mother Nature's best medicine. A balm for hurt minds. The local elders call it Mellow Fruitfulness."

Maggie tries to suppress a laugh. "Sounds out of season."

"Out of season?"

"Yes. 'Ode to Autumn'? By Keats? 'Season of mists and mellow fruitfulness'?"

"I don't read enough poetry. Another weakness? Maybe. But I feel poetry appeals to the intellect. And I distrust intellectual pursuits." Ms. Deepmere takes a drag and blows a series of expanding smoke rings toward the window. "What little success I enjoy, I owe to the nature gods. Well, nature and *this* contraption. Makes quite a racket. Annoys the hell out of my colleagues, but I refuse to dictate to an IMP. This hunk of metal is as high-tech as I'll ever get." She leans over the desk and, with her index fingers, hammers away at the keys of her typewriter. "Turns writing into a physical act. Almost a violent one. Absolute murder on your wrists. But all technology, even something as simple as a typewriter, comes at a cost. A couple of sore wrists, that's as much as I'm willing to pay. An IMP would rob me of time well spent staring out this window. But now isn't the time for daydreaming. Adventure calls."

Ms. Deepmere taps her wristwatch, an antique like the typewriter, and scrambles the hands.

"It's not an adventure unless you lose all track of time." She grabs her jeans jacket from the back of the chair. "Let's hit the road. If this festival is half as good as you say it is, I'll be sure to acknowledge you in my new book. Your brother, too. Next time, ask him to join us. I bet we'd all have a far-out trip. Real far-out."

Thirty-Six

Unwilling to ride with someone who has been smoking cannabis, Maggie insists on taking the helm during the first leg of the trip. Before firing up the ignition, she takes a moment to admire the 1957 Plymouth Fury's professionally polished bone-white finish, its gleaming chrome trim restored to its original brilliance. Maggie, who rarely leaves campus and has never had the pleasure of driving an antique car, grips the wheel tightly with both hands and maneuvers through heavy traffic. She cringes every time a transport thunders by in the passing lane, the black glass of its driverless cab bearing down on them with robotic indifference.

"Don't worry," says Ms. Deepmere. "This car is fully equipped with all of the mandatory safety features. The transmission has been acting up a bit, but this is a machine, after all. I mean, a *real* machine. The kind with moving parts."

At the city walls, Maggie stops to present identification to the officer standing guard. Few classic cars are permitted to burn fossil fuels, and Maggie wonders how Ms. Deepmere can afford the exorbitant fees. The guard, wearing a name patch that reads Sgt. Stanpole, lowers his aviator sunglasses, leans over to look in the rear window, and spots the IMP hovering above the back seat. He never looks at Ms. Deepmere in the passenger seat or asks about the overpowering smell of Mellow Fruitfulness wafting from the windows. Maggie stares straight ahead, her heart racing, and maintains a rigid silence. She has every legal right to bring the IMP, and the guard has no reason to detain them. This doesn't stop the officer from walking around the car and scanning the tags. After five excruciating minutes, he tells her to drive safely and waves them through the gate. Maggie accidentally hits the gas before putting the car in drive and fills the guardhouse with an asphyxiating cloud of blue exhaust.

She pulls the shifter, and the Fury lurches forward.

With each passing mile, she grows more confident driving the Fury and tries to remember if she's been in an automobile like this before. After an hour, they exit the interstate and travel down a two-lane road. Abandoned suburbs soon give way to a vast rolling prairie where tall grasses and wildflowers have reclaimed endless acres of corn and soybeans. There are no farmhouses here or grain silos, no billboards or high-tension power lines, no signs pointing the way to a clean and brightly lit restroom, nothing except the road itself to suggest the familiarity of civilization. Maggie knows it's only a matter of time before she'll need to stop, and she doesn't want to squat like an animal on the side of the road. She also isn't sure she can trust the IMP to watch for the painted faces that might be peering from behind a solitary willow or lurking in a grove of hickories.

Ms. Deepmere looks at her. "Think we'll see them?"

"See who?"

"The Star Throwers. The Forest Dwellers. The Watchers. The Travelers. We have to pass through their territory to reach the festival. The schismatics usually keep away from surveilled areas during the day, but they've been known to set up blockades at dusk. We should be fine as long as we reach our destination before nightfall. Naturally, your friend back there will give us any updates if the situation changes?" Ms. Deepmere turns and glances at the IMP. "It doesn't say an awful lot, does it? Looks like it's in sleep mode."

"Please, Ms. Deepmere, not this again."

"Not what again?"

"You were going to ask if I think it dreams."

"Actually, I was going to ask your opinion of the schismatics. A strange way of life. I mean, living out here, free from social institutions. It's hard to imagine. No schools, no corporations, no banks, no courts, no governments, no organized religion. I wonder if it's liberating. Or terrifying."

"They still have families," Maggie says. "Families are institutions, too."

"Aren't families a part of the natural order of things?"

"There's nothing natural about living in the wild."

Having rejected the creature comforts of modern civilization, the schismatics live hand to mouth. Many are led by women who dare call themselves enchantresses or by charismatic men declaring themselves mighty chieftains, but Maggie cannot fathom why so many adults subject their children to a life of privation and tribalism. According to the news alerts, more people than ever before are fleeing the cities, and an entire generation of children has already gone feral. With their long, knotted hair and fresh initiatory scars covering their torsos, the young schismatics grunt and whistle to one another and throw stones at wary travelers. Most have never been taught to read, write, or perform basic calculations. Indeed, many have never seen pen and paper. Nevertheless, troupes of boys and girls scout the hinterland, foraging for food. They carve mysterious signs in trees and paint indecipherable symbols on lonely roadways — crude mandalas and huge solar discs with radiating arms.

"I have an idea!" says Ms. Deepmere. "We should pull over and do a little mushroom hunting."

"Mushroom hunting?" Maggie repeats with a look of glazed incomprehension.

"I can spot a blue halo or liberty cap a mile away. I used to date a brilliant homeopath who taught me how to identify dozens of different species. A skinny little neurotic man with mommy issues. I used to find him alone in his greenhouse, whispering to his potted plants. From the way he tilted his head close to the shoots and leaves, he seemed to think the plants were talking to him. When we split up, I permanently borrowed some of his notebooks." Ms. Deepmere points. "Open the glove compartment. Go on, open it."

Maggie hesitates. Ms. Deepmere strikes her as the kind of person who, just for laughs, might set a mousetrap on top of the registration and insurance card. Taking care not to disturb anything, she delicately opens the latch and reaches inside.

"This?" she asks.

Ms. Deepmere nods. "Take a peek."

Maggie unties the leather straps and thumbs through detailed sketches of plants with names she's never heard. Trout lily. Wild geranium. Round-lobed Hepatica. Spring beauty. There are also drawings of toadstools, puffballs, stinkhorns, and earthstars. The handwriting is neat and precise, the complex chemical formulae filling entire pages.

"Most scientists say there's no such thing as magic," says Ms. Deepmere. "To them, it's inconceivable that plants can think, can make logical deductions." She rests her elbow on the open window and surveys the landscape, her eyes half-closed in the glare. "But not my little homeopath. And certainly not the Star Throwers or the Forest Dwellers. The schismatics are disciples of some hermit woman who lived not far from here. They believe trees and plants are sentient and that mushrooms are guides to the spirit world. I've come around to their way of thinking. Lately, I get the impression that plants possess consciousness and that they communicate indirectly with other intelligent beings. On the weekends, I brew small pots of mushroom tea. I start slow, take small sips until the desired effect is achieved. I've learned a lot from fungi. They tell me that, for some people, the human body is a desolate way station; for others, it's a point of departure. I once stared for over an hour at the sunlight playing on the leaves outside my office window. That's when I began to suspect existence is a hypnotic light show, no more real than a film flickering through a movie projector. You know what those are? Have you ever seen a movie?"

"A long time ago," Maggie says. "At a museum, I think. With my brother. We were very young."

"A good movie can seem so convincing. All of those performers up there on the big screen, acting out a gripping drama. But of course, the actors aren't really there. They're projections. A beam of light flickering through the theater, scenes that vanish like forgotten tableaux. Yes, we should definitely stop and pick mushrooms. Bring them to the music festival. Sure beats the synthesized junk everyone uses today."

Maggie, who no longer takes her morning microdose of psilocybin, not after the technical error a few months ago when the IMP miscalculated the proper dosage, says, "We can't stop! I mean, the festival is an inappropriate venue for that sort of thing."

"Inappropriate? But it's called Rock My Soul. The soul is a deep thing. The deepest thing imaginable. Without a little guidance from Mother Nature, how can mere mortals hope to reach something so far down in the depths?"

"Divine grace?" Maggie says.

"Is that a rhetorical question?"

Maggie says nothing and stares at the road as it stretches on and on until it vanishes over a gentle hill on the horizon.

Thirty-Seven

"In their season, the grass grows and the flowers bloom, but the Word endures forever."

Somewhere under the hiss and static of the radio, a passionate preacher describes a celestial light and a door standing open in heaven, but just as his words take on even greater intensity, each breathless syllable building momentum, he goes suddenly silent. Maggie grips the wheel and tries to ignore her growing discomfort. Another hour has come and gone, and she's beginning to worry. At some point, they must pass a town with a clean restroom. Ms. Deepmere tries adjusting the knobs when the preacher speaks again. He sounds different now, his carefully modulated voice mimicking the style and manner of a disinterested newscaster.

"This just in. According to sources in the nation's capital, America is one step closer to ratifying a new constitutional amendment, the first in nearly twenty years. Moments ago, the legislatures of all fifty-two states indicated their near-unanimous support for the measure. If ratified, the proposed amendment would place strict limits on general artificial intelligence and the private use of IMPs. Despite continued progress, a small but vocal minority of citizens continue to express serious concerns about..."

Ms. Deepmere switches off the radio. "I can't stand politics. How long has this amendment been in the works anyway? Three years? Four? 'An AI may never do what human beings are capable of doing for themselves.' Kind of draconian, isn't it? Your IMP must be getting pretty nervous. No more battery charges for you, right, old buddy?"

Ms. Deepmere tries to pat the IMP like a dog, but it backs away from her reach.

"I meant to ask what you're studying at Aspern. You into antique robots or something? The history of artificial intelligence? What interests you? What's your calling?"

"I'm not sure I'd describe it as my calling," Maggie says, a bit irritated by the tenor of the question, "but I just published an essay in *Conclusions & Completeness: the Journal of Gilded Age Studies*. It's only ten pages, but my professors tell me I have a future as a scholar."

"*Conclusions & Completeness*? Hell, I used to subscribe to that pretentious rag. No offense. What's the title of your essay?"

"'International Episodes: The Real and Surreal in the "High" Middle Period.'"

"No shit? I've read it! Let's see if I can remember. You argue that an uninspired Henry James, terrified at the prospect of reinventing his style to suit the sensibilities of 20th-century readers, experienced a serious spiritual crisis."

"Impressive," says Maggie. "That's practically a direct quote from the abstract."

"I have a photographic memory. In spite of all the reefer. Or maybe because of it. Now let me see." Ms. Deepmere frowns with the effort of recollection and then brightens slightly. "Yes, as I recall, James was upset by a conversation with that upstart H.G. Wells. *The Time Machine* had caused quite a sensation. James thought science fiction was just another fad, something for strange children who liked to play with electric wires in their parents' cellars. Felt that way ever since he was a young novelist and had a heated discussion with Jules Verne in one of those fashionable salons on the Rue de Bretagne in Paris."

"That's right," Maggie says. "James and Wells were introduced at a party in London. Wells is rumored to have mocked James for writing silly ghost stories. 'What are ghosts, sir, but a convenient 19th-century substitute for visitors from another time and dimension?' As you might imagine, Wells' comment didn't sit well with him. All his life, James had a serious preoccupation with the spirit world. Not to mention an obsession with neurotic nannies and troubled society women. He also had a delicate ego easily wounded by criticism. In fact, this conversation so unnerved him that he spiraled into a depression and began experimenting with nitrous oxide. Under his brother William's strict medical supervision, of course."

Ms. Deepmere smiles. "So Henry enjoyed a little laughing gas, did he?"

"Some scholars have made that claim. But I'm not sure he enjoyed it per se. Between fits of wild laughter and sustained bouts of inconsolable sobbing, he threatened to hop on a train and go out west."

Ms. Deepmere laughs. "I'd bet money big brother put that fool idea into his head. Hell, William probably offered to join him in the territories. But I doubt those two dandies would have made it further west than Ohio. Just think how that would have changed the course of American letters. Hank and Billy James, a pair of badass literary outlaws, setting up shop in a boomtown brothel along one of the towpath canals. While Billy psychoanalyzed broken-down old whores in the back rooms, Hank would sit quietly on the porch and crank out dime-store adventure novels about busted-up barge captains and brawling canal workers. I can picture it. Henry James, riding sidesaddle along a bridle path, his unshaven jowls powdered in the dust of the road."

"Yes, that's a funny idea." Maggie glowers when Ms. Deepmere reaches into her pocket and fires up another fat stick of Mellow Fruitfulness. "Is it true that William James is one of your influences?"

"In a way," Ms. Deepmere answers, moistening the blunt with her lips. "When I was starting out, I tried my hand at scholarship. If you want a full-time position at a university, you need to publish esoteric nonsense in the proper magazines and journals. But I learned long ago that I'm no good at the university game. Academics distrust my methodology."

"Your methodology?"

"I'm a necromancer, didn't you know? That's the allegation, anyway. I have this knack, you see, for bringing back the dead. And nothing terrifies a rationalist more than a woman who raises spirits."

Thirty-Eight

At last, they come to a small outpost, an old midwestern factory town judging by the brick warehouses and clapboard houses crowding the grid of streets. A rusted pickup truck, at least as old as the Fury, swerves into their lane, its mudflaps flashing lewd silhouettes of reclining ladies.

Maggie jerks the wheel hard to the left and reads the weather-beaten sign at the side of the road. "Welcome to Heavenly Hill. Isn't that the village's name in *Burn Your Life Down*?"

But Ms. Deepmere is snoring in the passenger seat, her head lolling from side to side, her dry mouth sucking at the air, her right hand dusted in ashy Mellow Fruitfulness.

They pass a deconsecrated church converted in recent years to a café. From its belfry hangs a banner announcing plans for a nature walk to commemorate Earth Day. Below the spire, nested on a narrow ledge, a hawk gazes over the square and waits for a squirrel, a chipmunk, or even a sick cat to cross its path. Maggie whispers the names of the retail shops that ring the square. The Time Warp, The Cosmic Serpent, The Galactic Gallery, The Crystal Palace. Not far from a fountain where a little boy pitches pennies, she parks the Fury at a meter.

Without waiting for her IMP, she jumps from the car and says, "Nature calls!"

She dashes across the street to Book Your Trip, a store that specializes in used and rare books, but when she enters the shop, Maggie sees an eclectic array of items — vinyl records with psychedelic album covers; tentacled glass bongs with the heads of bug-eyed extraterrestrials; framed lithographs of lunar landscapes and inhospitable exoplanets; huge hunks of purple quartz and magnetized iron; hand-carved Himalayan salt lamps; exotic plant oils reputed to have medicinal properties.

Behind the sales counter, enthroned in a lawn chair with faded blue webbing, the proprietor sits with his eyes closed, his hands on the armrests, the heels of his snakeskin boots resting on a makeshift footstool of antiquated textbooks on genetics and computer engineering. With his wild white hair spilling over his shoulders and a pair of reading glasses resting on the bridge of his nose, he looks part librarian, part gunslinger, and not particularly happy to have a stranger disrupt the solitude of his dusty dominion — but then strangers are resented everywhere.

Maggie approaches the counter and quietly says, "Excuse me, sir? I was wondering if I could use —"

Without cracking an eye, the man says, "Restroom is for paying customers only."

"I understand, but you see, we've been on the road —"

"Isn't a rest stop." Showing no inclination to rise from his chair, he rubs his eyes and scratches his chin. His nails are black with dirt, and his beard grows in patches on his pale cheeks.

"But, sir, I really need to —"

"Gotta buy something first."

Through years of prayer and disciplined meditation, Maggie has learned to reject mindless consumerism, but this is an emergency, and she isn't in the mood for an unpleasant confrontation with a sharp-tongued townie who has a taste for cheap beer and demolition derbies.

Exasperated, she turns from the counter and marches down one of the aisles. At the back of the store, she sees a circle of chairs as if the proprietor hosts the occasional book discussion groups. Maybe in a town named Heavenly Hill, the people gather here for weekly bible study, and it gives her some hope that on the cluttered shelves she'll find a book of psalms or a verse from the gospels. "It's easier for a camel to pass through the eye of a needle than a rich man to enter the Kingdom of God." Maggie has often wondered what the Lord meant when

He used the word "rich." By any metric, even the poorest American has more creature comforts than the mightiest kings of medieval Europe. Does this mean everyone is condemned to remain outside the heavenly gates for all eternity? Was there no possibility of redemption?

Against the back wall, Maggie finds an odd assortment of science fiction comic books and used paperbacks on the paranormal — UFOs, spirit animals, telepathy. One tome purports to be the first serious study of the mystical practices and body modifications of the schismatics. Another tells the story of Gwendolyn Greene and her dog McKenna. Historic personages. Names that ring a bell but that she can't quite place.

Near the front of the store, she sees flying saucer keychains, rocket-ship ballpoint pens, and small, lime-green alien babies with broad domed foreheads, pinwheel eyes, and bright blue antennae. As a gift for Ms. Deepmere, she grabs a dashboard figurine, a dog dressed as an astronaut, its wide toothy grin beaming from behind the glass shield of a space helmet.

"Will that be all for you today?" the proprietor asks without meeting her gaze.

"Yes."

He brushes a piece of grit from the scuffed toe of one boot. "Care for a free brochure? Has a list of restaurants and shops."

"We're not staying long."

"Where headed? East or west?"

"South."

"South?"

His sleepy eyes suddenly come into sharp focus when he finally looks at her. He rises slowly from the chair, his knees popping, his jeans hanging from his bony hips, and regards her in a curious way. It's almost as though he's frightened of her.

"No paved roads that way," he says. "No towns either. Only thing you'll find is Lost Village Canyon." He whistles and makes a hand gesture like a car flying into the abyss. "We've had some heavy rain these last few days. Most of the trails, if you can call them trails, have been washed away. Pockets of quicksand out there, too."

"We'll be careful," Maggie says.

The proprietor shakes his head. "No, sweetie, I don't think you understand."

"Please don't call me 'sweetie.'"

His mouth snaps shut. He nervously adjusts the pencil and notepad in his shirt pocket. "Just trying to help is all."

She pushes the space dog across the counter. "How much do I owe you?"

"How much? Hmm, let's see." He rubs his forehead. "Eighty credits."

"Eighty!"

"Or you could just give me forty in cash. Everyone knows we're all gonna need hard currency in the coming days."

Maggie reaches into her spring jacket and shakes her head.

"I'm sorry, but I seem to have left my PERTINENCE card in the car."

The proprietor snatches the space dog from the counter.

"If you'll give me a minute —"

Behind her, the door opens, then swings closed with a sharp clap. A boy, perhaps nine or ten years old, stands at the entrance. Behind him, the IMP casts a silver glow above his head. The child wears hiking boots and a camouflage backpack. His fingernails are filthy, his hair tangled and knotted, and he smells of woodsmoke and sweat as if he's been camping for weeks in the wilderness.

"Hey, did anyone lose an IMP?"

The proprietor stumbles backward. "What did I tell you about those damned things!"

The boy winces. "But someone left it outside."

The proprietor slams a hand down on the counter. "Is that my concern? Get it out of here. Now!"

"Don't raise your voice," Maggie says. "The IMP belongs to me."

"To *you*?" The proprietor glances around the shop and then looks at Maggie with something like pity. "Well … you're just going to have to leave it outside."

The boy nudges Maggie with a scabby elbow and places a plastic squirt gun on the counter. "Would you buy this for me, Mommy? I need a new ray-gun to scare off the poachers stealing from our garden."

"What did you call me?" Maggie asks.

"Don't bother my customers!" the proprietor says.

"He's not bothering me."

The boy grabs the squirt gun from the counter and races from the store.

"Hey! Get your ass back here!" He rushes from the behind the counter and thrusts his head from the door. "Is this how your generation treats its elders? One day, you'll discover devils only beget more devils. And society has a way of dealing with devils!"

He returns the register.

"Well, I apologize for that. He's wild, that one. Like a badly behaved dog."

"I'm happy to pay full price for the figurine and the squirt gun," Maggie says. "The IMP has access to my PERTINENCE account."

His face once again taking on the jaundiced pallor of a defeated man deep in drink, the proprietor tosses the space dog into a brown paper bag. He must have kept a bottle hidden among the lopsided stacks surrounding him.

"You still need to use the restroom?" he mutters, gazing out the picture window.

"Yes, please."

He jerks his thumb at the door behind the counter. "Back there. And don't make a mess. I just cleaned it."

Maggie hurries around the corner, but before entering the restroom, she spies the proprietor sinking back into his chair and speaking to the IMP. He mutters a string of obscenities and gestures irritably to the exit. The IMP spins above the countertop and casts colorful confetti across the ceiling before hovering out the door.

Thirty-Nine

Holding the brown paper bag from her fingertips like a dirty tissue and feeling like someone has just picked her pockets, Maggie walks toward the square and wonders why fate has sent her to such a peculiar place. She detests having to buy anything she doesn't need or want, and she can't understand why so many people live in constant fear that they may lose the relatively inconsequential things they already possess. They seem to operate under the misapprehension that this world, with all its pain and sorrow, is the only one they'll ever know. With such a grim worldview, is it any wonder they attempt to assuage their misery by collecting useless trinkets? Like this space dog. Maggie isn't sure why she chose it. Dogs frighten her, even small ones, and Ms. Deepmere has never mentioned owning a pet.

Still rattled by the encounter, she hurries along the sidewalk and spots Ms. Deepmere sitting on a park bench near a strange modernist sculpture made entirely from old bicycle parts, the baby blue frame gone to rust, the handlebars twisted and tarnished.

Behind an elm tree near the fountain, the little boy suddenly appears and creeps up behind Ms. Deepmere. He points his new squirt gun at the back of her head, and before Maggie can raise the alarm, the boy fires five or six rounds in quick succession. Shocked by the blast of cold water striking her neck and running down her back, Ms. Deepmere leaps from the bench and chases her assailant across the green. She stumbles on a branch and, giving a loud cry, falls face-first into a flowerbed reeking of fresh mulch.

The boy looks over his shoulder and laughs. "Have a nice trip?"

Outraged by this behavior, Maggie marches across the square.

"You! Apologize this instant!"

Like a skilled duelist, the boy twirls the plastic pistol on one finger, then holsters it in the back pocket of his camouflage cargo shorts.

Ms. Deepmere limps back to the bench and massages her ankle.

"Wasn't a fair fight, kid," she says, wiping her neck. "Shooting an unsuspecting civilian like that. In the back, no less."

"I wanted to warn you," Maggie says.

Ms. Deepmere snaps her fingers. "I have an idea! Why don't you gimme that squirt gun and let me take a shot at you?"

"It's a ray-gun!" he corrects her.

"Oh, I see. A *ray*-gun."

Standing at a safe distance near the swings, the boy spins on his heels and blasts a pigeon, a mural of a legendary woman named Hilda Whitby, a colony of ants marching in single file between the cracks in the cement sidewalk. Crouching low to the ground, looking left and right as if for enemy combatants, the boy maneuvers between shrubs and makes his way to the fountain.

"You still haven't apologized," Maggie says.

The boy refills his gun and says, "Sorry, I didn't realize you were friendlies. But now that you're here, can you provide transportation? It's a long walk back to the Mothership, and the next personnel carrier doesn't leave until dusk."

The boy throws his backpack to the ground, unzips the top compartment, and finds a blue bandana buried under a dozen candy wrappers. He wipes down the gun and stuffs the bandana back in his bag.

"I think," Ms. Deepmere says to Maggie, "that our little space cadet is asking for a ride home."

"You shouldn't accept rides from strangers," Maggie tells him. "If you need a ride, you should call your parents."

"They're not home right now."

"Where are they?"

The boy thinks about this before answering. "They're seeking peace of mind."

Maggie sighs. "What's your name?"

"Sirius." He puts the gun barrel in his mouth and squeezes the trigger. "Like the star. 2.64 parsecs from Earth. Moving closer to our solar system every day."

"What's your *real* name."

"That *is* my real name. So will you do it?"

"Do what?"

"Take me back to the Mothership?"

"Well, I suppose we can't just leave you here."

"Hear that, space cowboy?" Ms. Deepmere says with a strained smile. Gripping the bench, she stands gingerly on her sprained ankle. "The captain has just granted permission to come aboard our ship. But we're on a mission, too, and we'd like to reach our destination before the dog star rises. Let's get going. Time to blast off."

"Lead the way. I'll cover you!"

The boy raises his ray-gun, prepared at the slightest provocation to fire on enemy combatants. Ms. Deepmere drapes an arm around Maggie's shoulder for support and limps across the square.

On the street, the IMP circles the Fury and scares off a robin that tries to land on the hood. A police cruiser glides by and stops beside their vehicle. The officer speaks briefly to the IMP and then looks directly at Maggie. He scribbles something in a notebook. Still staring at her, he tips his cap and drives slowly away.

Forty

On the dashboard, the plastic space dog bobbles erratically as if inviting Maggie to play a friendly game of fetch. In the backseat, shouting confusing directions in her ear, their passenger scrambles around the backseat and gently bats the IMP like a helium balloon.

"I think it's low on oil or something," the boy says.

"Stop that," Maggie tells him. "It isn't a toy."

"Where'd you find this thing anyway? A junkyard?"

"It belonged to my brother —"

"Slow down! Take a left! Okay, now take a right at those trees. No, no, the *other* ones! The really tall ones. Now, follow this road for, like, a mile. Or maybe two. I'm not sure."

The road vanishes into the deep shadow of a tree tunnel, and the pavement abruptly gives way to gravel. No more than a cart track that fades into the stony ground, the road is barely wide enough to accommodate the Fury's whitewall tires. The car fishtails around an endless series of hairpin bends, the tires crushing loose pieces of shale and the fossilized bones of giant lizards, millions of years dead, and Maggie struggles to navigate the rough and rutted road. If the windshield is any indication, the surrounding woods are already swarming with insects. She weaves between thickets of bramble that threaten to scratch the paint job and craters deep enough to crack an axle.

"Are you sure we're heading in the right direction?"

"Keep going!"

Hunched on a dead limb, a turkey vulture feeds on the entrails of a ripe rabbit. The boy reaches for his ray-gun, lines up the barrel as best he can, closes one eye, and puts his finger on the trigger.

"Didn't I just tell you to keep your seatbelt buckled?" Maggie snaps.

The engine coughs and sputters, and the car bucks violently. The startled bird leaps away with a loud grunt and heavy flap of its wings. It sails over the treetops, screeching at them.

The boy flashes a petulant grin. "You made me miss! Did this personnel carrier come from the same junkyard as the IMP?"

"You're just a lousy shot, kid," Ms. Deepmere remarks. "But I admit the transmission could definitely use a tune-up. Don't like the way the engine is revving. No, I don't like it at all. Sounds expensive to fix. Costs a lot of money, these classic cars."

"Money is a superstition," the boy declares. "That's what my grandpa told me. It's not real. It's a social construct, a phantom, a puff of smoke. But people need to believe something. Even if deep down they know their beliefs are illusions."

"A wise man, your grandfather," says Ms. Deepmere. "But I'm as superstitious as it gets. A total crackpot. I believe very much in the specter of money. Guess I better publish more books. Or teach more classes."

"You're a schoolteacher? My grandpa says schools keep people in a state of ... of ... perpetual adolescence. I'll figure things out a lot faster on my own without sitting in a classroom and raising my hand to ask permission to use the bathroom. Travel, he tells me. It's the best education there is. With a transport like this, you probably haven't seen too much of the world. Worried all the time about being stranded, right? Hey, where's the propellor on this thing? Or does it use jet propulsion?"

"Do you get your sense of humor from your grandfather?" Maggie asks, growing increasingly irritated by the boy's lack of respect.

"I'm more or less forced to travel," Ms. Deepmere says. "I'm adjunct faculty. And an incurable graphomaniac."

The boy looks out the window, barely listening. "That's not a real word. Just like you're not real. I should know. I'm a prodigy. Everyone says so."

"In a town of mental defectives, that's not saying much. And I assure you, kid, I'm a real scribomaniac."

"What does *that* mean?"

"It means I'm disposable. Writers haven't made a strong case for books. I can't tell you how often I've given readings to a roomful of empty chairs. Sometimes, the humiliation is more than I can bear. And no one reads the greats anymore. Ballard, Borges, Bradbury. Let me ask you something, kid. You like reading books?"

"Books?" he scoffs. "I don't have time for books. I'm too busy patrolling our garden. I've caught schismatics trying to steal fruits and vegetables late at night. But they won't get away with it. Not anymore. I'll blast 'em with my ray-gun if they start coming around again this harvest!"

Ms. Deepmere turns to Maggie. "You hear the latest news at Aspern?"

"No, what?"

"Last week, the provost announced plans to allocate more funds to the College of Neuroscience and Advanced Consciousness Studies. Said the college is committed to serving the interests of students, not artists. Moving forward, the college will offer more courses in synaptic computation rather than creative writing."

"What does that mean for you?" Maggie asks.

"It means Aspern won't be renewing my contract at the end of the semester."

"What's wrong with this scrap heap?" The boy pushes the IMP away from his arm. "Is it gonna explode or something?"

Like an ambulance on its way to a terrible wreck, the IMP suddenly emits flashing red lights and fills the Fury's interior with a high-pitched alarm. For the brief time she's been in possession of it, Maggie has never known the IMP to behave this way. She slows the car and stops beside a vacant lot where the crumbling brick foundation of an old farmhouse protrudes from the weeds and ivy. Thick ribbons of dust curl through the open windows, shrouding the IMP and muting its pulsating lights. It pushes past the boy and floats out the back window.

"Now what the hell is it doing?" Ms. Deepmere asks.

The IMP hovers beside a lopsided sign, its bronze writing covered in a thick patina.

The boy jumps from the car and fires at a dragonfly drifting on the breeze.

As if in a trance, Maggie trudges through the undergrowth and clears away the tangled vines from the plaque.

"Some kind of historical marker. Says this was once the home of a dog named McKenna, an American hero and the pride of Heavenly Hill. In 1957, McKenna was selected to be the first animal to travel by rocket into outer space." Maggie runs a hand over the plaque and has the unmistakable impression that she's been here before. "Seems an unlikely birthplace for the first Yuri Gagarin or Alan Shepard."

The ruins trigger a sharply drawn scene from early childhood, one that feels like a distinct memory rather than a fleeting sense of déjà vu. Had she visited this place as a child? An infant? In a previous lifetime? In a future lifetime? Were such things possible? The flowers come back, and so do the leaves. Always the same but different.

"This is the old Greene place," the boy says, balancing on the crumbling limestone foundation.

"They say it's haunted. But it's like Grandpa always says. Everyone has their funny superstitions."

"There's a lake," Maggie whispers. "Right over there. I remember..."

The boy laughs. "There's no lake."

Maggie hurries through the grass and down a gentle slope, past the burned stump — lightning strike? forest fire? — of a giant oak tree. She pushes through scrub brush and bramble and stops at a limestone ridge that commands a panoramic view of a canyon where the silver back of a river carves a crooked path along steep shale cliffs.

"I swear ... there was a lake here."

The IMP, now pulsating a cautious orange-yellow, floats behind her.

"Government drained the lake a hundred years ago," the boy says, catching up with Maggie. "Scientists found a giant rock buried in the mud. They say it came from outer space. That's around the same time people started reporting strange lights in the sky."

Maggie stares into the canyon and softly says, "Why did you call me Mommy? Back at the store?"

"What? No, I didn't. You're weird!"

The boy dashes toward a trail that traverses the canyon walls.

"Anyway, I can't remember what my mommy looks like."

"Can't remember? Wait! Where are you going?"

"Thanks for the ride! I can walk from here."

"Walk? Where?"

"Down there. In the valley. That's where I live."

"You *walked* into town from the bottom?"

Ms. Deepmere, wincing with the effort of it, limps toward the ridge. In her greasy hands, she holds a rubber gasket. "Well, it's as bad as I thought. We're not going anywhere until we can send for a replacement."

"My grandpa keeps parts just like that in the storage shed behind the Mothership. Come with me. I'll show you."

Maggie crosses her arms. "Can't you see she's in no condition to hike down that path? Besides, there's quicksand in the canyon."

"Quicksand? Ha! What fool told you that? There's no quicksand. Come on, I'll give you a free tour of the Mothership."

"You hear that?" says Ms. Deepmere. "A free tour."

Maggie backs away from the ridge. "But your ankle…"

"I'll wait here for you."

"You want me to go by myself?"

"I'd hate for you to miss out on a new experience. Trust me on this. If you want to see anything interesting, you need to leave the car behind. Take the IMP if you'd like. Just to be safe."

"I don't think that's such a great idea."

"Look, maybe there's a reason you're here. Maybe there's a purpose behind it all. Maybe this is where you discover your true calling. The calling that's different from everyone else's." She plants her hands on Maggie's shoulders. "Because I believe you do have a calling. Oh, I apologize. Got grease all over your new spring coat. Don't worry. I'll pay to have it cleaned when you get back."

Forty-One

A longtime city dweller accustomed to alienating apartment blocks and crowded streets, Maggie plods along the path and listens to the unceasing drone of insects resurrected after an interminable winter sleep. Every few yards, a stone works its way into a shoe, forcing her to stop and shake it loose. A mistake. The moment she kneels to untie her laces, a mosquito lights on her shoulder, rubbing its forelegs and readying its proboscis in anticipation of a succulent meal. Maggie slaps the back of her neck and scratches furiously at her scalp. For a moment, she feels as though she has crash-landed on a remote alien world crawling with intelligent life. All of this buzzing and trilling, she realizes, is a sophisticated form of communication. The bugs are signaling the way to a food source, warning each other about an intruder, or trying to attract a mate.

Thirty minutes later, after reaching the canyon floor, she and the boy enter an untrammeled wilderness of second-growth forest. Beginning to sense the futility of this absurd expedition, she considers turning back, but she doesn't want to disappoint Ms. Deepmere.

Leaping effortlessly over uneven rocks like a mountain goat, the boy moves so far ahead that Maggie can no longer see him on the poorly marked trail. She hears only the distant crackle of dry leaves and the sharp snap of fallen branches. In an attempt to catch up to him, she smashes her toes against roots protruding like petrified snakes from the ground.

The ever-vigilant IMP, hovering protectively over her shoulder, urges her to keep moving.

For the next ten minutes, she steps daintily through pockets of mud, trembling at the thought of being swallowed alive. At one point, to regain the path, she straddles the trunk of a fallen oak and clumsily rolls into a trampled patch of weeds.

A few minutes later, she arrives at a murmuring brook that flows swiftly through sandy banks. The boy waits midstream in ankle-deep water and points to a hand-painted sign nailed to a birch on the opposite bank.

This Way to the Mothership!
Admission: Only 50 PERTINENCE Points
No Exceptions

Arms outstretched, he skips with confidence across a set of uneven stepping stones that span the stream. To make the crossing easier for Maggie, the IMP casts a bright beam on the sparkling granite rocks. Maggie hesitates. Terrified she might slip and be swept away, she hops from one slick rock to the next. At the halfway point, she manages to wedge the toe of her left shoe between two pieces of pink granite polished smooth by the stream. Trying not to panic, she extends her arms to maintain balance and yanks her foot free.

After an hour's journey, they ascend a long, gradual slope where the trees begin to thin. Maggie pauses to catch her breath. She rests her hands on her knees, and when she raises her eyes, she sees the boy striding through a large circular meadow bursting with wildflowers. Easily one hundred yards in circumference and bathed in warm afternoon light, the clearing is a tranquil pool of the brightest bluebells Maggie has ever seen. Everything seems perfectly arranged, as in a painting, so much so that she doesn't know where art ends and nature begins. Amazed by each kaleidoscopic display of violet-blue and lavender and every virtuosic trill of birdsong coming from the undulating grass, she wades across the meadow, her fingertips grazing the flower petals, her eyes fixed on the object in the center of the clearing, something at once familiar and incomprehensible.

"How long have you lived here?" she whispers.

"In the Mothership?" The boy stops and checks the ray-gun's water level. "I dunno. Since I was a baby, I guess." He shoots a beetle, a bumblebee, a butterfly. "You must've read about it in the brochures back in town."

"I didn't take a brochure."

"After that girl strapped the family dog to a rocket and tried blasting him into outer space, visitors started making the pilgrimage to Heavenly Hill. My grandpa thought he could make some quick cash if he bought a few acres and built the Mothership. Our ancestors were obsessed with aliens and UFOs. But people stopped coming to Heavenly Hill a long time ago. And no one ever visits the canyon. Not unless they're lost. But you're not lost, are you? You know exactly where you're going."

Maggie looks back at the IMP and says, "I've been here before, haven't I?"

The IMP spins counterclockwise and does a remarkably adept impression of a warbler's song.

In the center of the meadow, gleaming under the cloudless sky, a large silver saucer floats ten feet off the ground. Maggie takes a tentative step closer. With its retractable gangway and dozen oval windows, the spacecraft presides like a broken-down deity over the bluebells. Incompetently riveted together and slapped with a few coats of silver paint, it seems to be some kind of prefabricated fiberglass dwelling. Drawn inexorably into its orbit, Maggie circumambulates the saucer and realizes that it isn't hovering like the IMP but is fixed firmly to three iron beams anchored to three granite blocks. With each successive lap, she moves just a little closer to the gangway. It's like a tractor beam is tugging at her, but the closer she gets, the more comfortable she becomes, her mind clear and unburdened by worries.

"You need a place to stay tonight?" the boy asks. "Grandpa rents rooms. We used to have all kinds of interesting people stay with us. Like that mean handyman. And that science teacher who was always memorizing mathematical equations. Last summer, a lady calling herself a 'conceptual artist' stayed with us. She used to go around Heavenly Hill, looking for vintage bicycles. Managed to get her hands on a 1957 baby blue Schwinn. Cut it apart with a blowtorch and then welded the pieces back together again. It's on display in the town square. Looks like a rusty pretzel. She didn't know anything about gardening when she first came to the Mothership. But once she tasted our fresh fruits and vegetables, she learned to weed the flower boxes and prune the plants climbing the trellises. Never wanted to go back to eating the poison they serve in cities, that's for sure. Everything we eat comes from our garden, and we never have to spend any money on food. I'll show you!"

The boy races to a hedge on the other side of the meadow and disappears through a small opening. Maggie hesitates. Although service is limited beyond the city walls, she considers having the IMP summon a driverless pod to get her, but she'll likely have to wait for hours before one appears — and that's only if a pod can make its way down the treacherous switchbacks into the canyon.

"Come on! This way!"

Forty-Two

Divided into a precise grid of raised beds and perpendicular walkways of crushed stone, the garden encompasses an acre of land and, from what Maggie can tell, requires considerable care and attention. Each box is meticulously maintained and labeled, and around the garden's perimeter, NO TRESPASSING signs have been posted.

"Look at this!"

Inside a toolshed painted red to resemble an old barn, the boy shows Maggie a wheelbarrow, shovel, spade, rake, hoe, and pruning shears. Everything a person might need to cultivate a garden. But Maggie doesn't see the rubber gasket the boy promised. She does, however, spot dangling from a hook, a thin chain on which is fastened a small, silver anchor. This, too, means something, but she isn't sure what. Then she recalls how in even the loveliest of gardens, no matter how well-built its walls, a snake always manages to slither inside and hide among the trees.

"Need to keep the poachers away!"

The boy dashes from the toolshed and twirls through the garden, spraying the beds with his ray-gun.

"At night, they wear wooden animal masks and try to scare me with their bullroarers."

"Who does?"

"The Star Catchers and Forest Dwellers. In their villages, they have megaliths fifty feet tall. And stone altars. The Travelers even have a serpent mound. And the Bridge of Dreams."

Maggie, who hasn't eaten a thing since leaving campus this morning, drifts among the saplings and budding plants. Feeling light-headed, she leans against a young tree labeled *Ficus religiosa*. The IMP warns her that her blood sugar is low. Ever since discovering it in her brother's trunk, Maggie has relied on the IMP for just about everything. It knows her better than she knows herself and accurately predicts her moods and desires. Under normal circumstances, it delivers food and drink directly to her dorm at regular intervals throughout the day. It also sanitizes all of the surfaces in her room, checks her temperature, tracks her heart rate, and monitors her pupil dilation. It never lets her see anything she doesn't want to see or hear anything she doesn't want to hear.

"Bridge of Dreams?" Maggie says.

"It's not actually a bridge. It's a cave. Sealed up for hundreds of years. The Travelers discovered it. But they're very strict about who goes inside. Once a year, on the morning of the summer solstice, they choose one person to enter the cave. Don't know what's in there, but when the person comes out, she isn't the same anymore. The Travelers say it's like crossing a bridge into your dreams. Or your worst nightmares. Would you like to see the cave opening? It's just a few miles south of here."

"The schismatics keep to themselves," Maggie says. "They're hostile to outsiders. And to IMPs."

"No, they're not! I camp with them all the time. They taught me to hunt and fish."

"I thought they raided your garden?"

"Well ... it's a kind of game we play. But they do hate IMPs, that's true. You'll need to leave it here."

"Impossible. I programmed it to be no further than fifteen feet from me at all times. Besides, I need to get back to the Fury before the sun goes down. We're on our way to a music festival." She kneels beside a box marked *Amanita muscaria* and feels tempted to pop a cap into her mouth. With an unsteady hand, she wipes the sweat from her eyes. "Do you have something I could eat? Anything at all. An apple, maybe?"

"We have lots of food in the Mothership. Follow me!"

"Let's go," she hisses.

But the IMP does not respond to her command. Rather than a gelatinous membrane, it now looks like a polished steel ball that begins to sink beneath the flowers until it hovers a few inches above the ground. She places her fingertips on the lifeless orb and gently pushes it through the hedge and into the meadow.

"The amendment has been ratified," it robotically repeats. "The amendment has been ratified."

"Stay here then. See what I care."

At the risk of being transported to a place she doesn't wish to go, Maggie approaches the Mothership and climbs the gangway. She stands outside the oval door the boy has left ajar and, for a moment, looks out over the meadow as if it's the last time she'll see the Earth again.

Forty-Three

She steps into a windowless storage room bathed in vernal green light. At first, she worries the boy has brought her to a top-secret lab to view a collection of alien lifeforms floating in jars of formaldehyde. Once her eyes adjust to the light, she realizes the mason jars, neatly labeled and alphabetically arranged on the floor-to-ceiling shelves, are filled with turnips, tomatoes, pickled beets, and carrots, enough rations to last a family an entire year. There are jugs of mead, too, and oak casks of wine and whisky.

"Up here!"

Resisting the urge to twist open a jar and use her fingers to scoop a handful of raspberry preserves into her mouth, Maggie follows the boy's voice up a spiral staircase and enters a spacious living area. To her astonishment, the Mothership's interior looks more like a frontier farmhouse than a poorly staged spaceship. While the large oval windows allow for abundant natural light and offer a stunning three-hundred-sixty-degree view of the meadow, the wood beams and hardwood floors make the saucer feel dark and enclosed, like a hermit's cave. At the center of the saucer, there's a wood stove and black chimney pipe, and instead of electric lamps, the occupants of the Mothership rely on oil lamps and brass lanterns. The kitchen has a cast iron oven and a large single-basin porcelain sink. She also notices a dozen or more walking sticks leaning against the wall and books scattered across the floor.

"I thought you didn't like to read," Maggie says, tiptoeing around a pillar of astronomy textbooks.

The boy searches the cupboards. "What? Oh, those. Grandpa is always bringing books home from the store. Trying to educate me on his own. He thinks we'll find answers to life's important questions. But books are a dead end. The human intellect will get you no closer to the truth than money."

"Is he here?"

"Who?"

"Your grandfather."

"Of course not. You think he can fly or something?"

On the coffee table, an enormous leather-bound dictionary catches Maggie's eye. She flips through the brittle, yellow pages and skims the faded, antique script until she finds the offending word.

im·pe·tus

/ˈimpədəs/

noun

- a force that makes something happen.

"Imp," she learns, is derived from an Old English word meaning "young shoot," which in turn is derived from a Greek word meaning "to implant," or more correctly, "to bring forth and make grow." Somewhere along the way, the word changed meaning until, at some point in the hazy and superstitious past, people began using it to describe a small, mischievous sprite. Or a little devil. Maggie chooses to think of her IMP as a trickster. With promises of meeting long-lost friends, the IMP convinced her to embark upon this foolish quest to attend Rock Your Soul.

With a loud yawn, she sinks into a recliner near the wood stove. For some reason, she feels perfectly at peace here, calm, clear-headed, untroubled by past or future, and decides there's no hurry to get back to the Fury. She leans back in the recliner and raises the footrest. Unused to so much physical exertion, she feels her eyes growing heavy. As the sun sinks below the canyon's eastern rim, she half expects the Mothership, commandeered by the little boy, to lift off the ground and fly away into the pink and purple clouds.

Fighting off sleep, she says, "Mind if I rest for a minute?"

"Rest as long as you'd like," the boy says from the kitchen.

"Someone should look after you until your grandfather comes home."

"You can stay the night if you want. Or the week. Or even the rest of the year. You can live here with us! We have lots of room. And we love company."

Forty-Four

Instead of visions of outer space, Maggie dreams of a frontier woman in a ragged black dress standing in the doorway of an old country inn. In the triptych of mirrors above a dressing table, she gazes at the endless replicas of herself. The woman pulls back the Candlewick bedspread and rests her head against the pillows. She falls asleep and dreams of a girl in a rowboat who gazes at her distorted reflection on the rippling water. While drifting across the lake, the girl falls asleep and, in turn, dreams of Maggie walking through the meadow of bluebells. Dreams within dreams. An infinite loop. This phantasmagoria continues until a familiar voice calls her name.

She jumps from the recliner. The sun has gone down, and Maggie panics at the darkness beyond the windows.

"I apologize. Didn't mean to startle you."

In the kitchen, ladling lentil stew into two wooden bowls, stands the proprietor of Book Your Trip.

"How did you know my name?" Maggie asks.

"My grandson informed me that we had a visitor. I'm Enoch. But I expect he told you that after you met in my shop." He gestures to the small table near one of the oval windows. "Dinner is ready. Hope you have a big appetite. I know I do. Damn strenuous hike from town. My knees are killing me."

"Where is he? Your grandson."

"On Saturday nights, he camps with the Travelers." Enoch places the bowls on the table, along with silverware and a pair of checkered cloth napkins. "Some day, in the not-too-distant future, the Travelers will ask to initiate the boy. After that, I probably won't see much of him. Come sit down before your stew gets cold."

Compared to their initial encounter earlier today at Book Your Trip, the proprietor is gracious and hospitable. In addition to the delicious stew, he serves chickpea pancakes and thick slices of warm bread with honey butter. He pours mead into his mug and speaks in a slow, deliberate manner.

"Thought I might do some business at the store, it being Earth Day and all, but you were my only customer." He sips his mead and says, "Glad you like it."

Maggie, chewing ravenously on a crust, nods and dabs her lips with a napkin. "Oh, yes, the bread is so fresh. And this stew is amazing. So many peas and carrots. I'll need to get your recipe."

"Not my best batch, but still pretty good. Everything's from our garden, including the bay leaves and fennel."

"Yes, he tells me you have the occasional guest who helps with the garden."

"Not recently. You're our first visitor in months."

"My friend is a novelist. I bet she'd like to rent a room if one is available. Seems like an ideal place to write. She's waiting back at the car. You must have seen her at the trailhead. She's probably worried sick about me."

Enoch shakes his head. "Didn't see anyone. Though I did see your IMP out there in the meadow."

"Are you sure? A woman in a white Plymouth Fury?"

"What's her name, this friend of yours?"

"Juliana Deepmere."

Enoch holds the mug to his lips but doesn't drink. "Deepmere, did you say?"

"We had engine problems. I came here to get a spare part. Do you suppose she walked back to town?"

"Juliana Deepmere?"

"Yes."

"Lady who writes gritty crime dramas? Likes being photographed holding shotguns and bottles of bourbon?"

"You know her work then?"

Enoch sets his mug on the table and leans forward in his chair.

"I do," he says, looking at her more intensely, "I've read a few of her books. But I'm a simple man, you see, unlike my clever grandson. I don't go in for astrophysics and radio astronomy. I've never known a boy to read so much."

"He told me you're a voracious reader."

"Boy likes to play games with our guests. And your IMP, I'm afraid, has been playing a trick on you, too."

"What do you mean? What kind of trick?"

He gives her a sympathetic smile.

"May I show you something?"

"Is anything wrong?"

"No, but I believe a different perspective might be helpful. Come with me."

Forty-Five

Maggie follows Enoch to the opposite end of the Mothership and watches him climb a metal ladder. He turns a handle to open a small hatch in the ceiling and hoists himself through the opening. As if guided by a different version of herself, one who has been through this experience before, Maggie climbs the rungs. Enoch offers his hand and helps her to the saucer's sloping roof.

She walks to the flat center and casts her eyes around the meadow. Fireflies blink in the clearing. A bat corkscrews across the sky. A doe and three spotted fawns scatter into the night. Maggie comes from a city that, when it isn't covered in clouds, is so polluted by artificial light that she has seen only a fraction of constellations, but now, standing in this dark valley, she can see more stars in the sky than she ever thought possible and can detect the Earth's slow rotation. Rather than feeling small and laughably inconsequential against the vastness of space, she begins to understand for the first time how connected she is to everything.

Enoch points to a cluster of stars.

"Canis Major. And that bright star over there, that's Sirius. The dog that never fails to catch what it's hunting. My grandson insists there's intelligent life out there. Says he can detect signals. A coded language. I hope the boy will take over the store for me one day, but let's face it. He isn't suited to a conventional lifestyle. School, college, a steady job. So many of our institutions seem designed to crush children like him."

Maggie hears the distant voices of a female chorus. The voices grow in volume before subsiding into the nocturnal sounds of the forest.

"The Travelers," Enoch says. "They don't tolerate books. Or IMPs. My grandson used to own one. Brought it with him when he came here to live with me after his mother passed away. That was, oh, five years ago now. At the time, I didn't have anything against IMPs. Thought they were dumber than goats. Dumber than deer. But this one made a good companion for the boy. In fact, after a few months, I started to enjoy having it around. Then, one day, while the boy was out exploring the trails, I decided to bring the IMP with me to the store. It's three miles each way, and the IMP kept me company by projecting holograms of historical personages from our small town. Hilda Whitby, Gwendolyn Greene. I had no idea the holograms could interact so convincingly with me. A miracle of technology, or so I thought."

He turns his eyes toward the moon shining above the treetops and shudders.

"On my way home that night, along a lonely stretch of trail, the IMP projected an image of my daughter. She spoke to me. Told me how much she loved me. Then she rested her head on my shoulder. I think I screamed. I can't be sure."

He shakes his head and pours himself more mead.

"Well! I picked up a good, sturdy branch and smashed the IMP to bits. If it could fool me, it could certainly fool McKenna, and I worried the boy might form an unhealthy bond with that dangerous contraption. I wasn't going to let that happen. And that's why I don't allow IMPs aboard the Mothership or inside my store. Earlier today, when I saw you standing at the counter, I thought your IMP was playing tricks on me. It's uncanny how much you look like my daughter. Even fooled my grandson for a minute. But then we all have a difficult time distinguishing reality from virtual reality."

Maggie searches for his eyes in the dark and whispers, "What is it you're trying to say?"

"People get easily confused, that's all. But you're an intelligent young woman. You must know that Juliana Deepmere is a pseudonym for an obscure writer who died in Heavenly Hill fifty years ago. That woman who joined you on your journey? She isn't real. She's an illusion. A high-tech hologram. And the only reason she isn't here right now is because your IMP is in the meadow. A good place for it, too. Not that it can do us much harm. Not anymore."

Maggie hears it again, the haunting female chorus floating on the wind.

"The Travelers sing when the moon is full. We live in a truly weird world. Best thing to do is accept the paradoxical nature of life."

Maggie nods and says softly, "My brother believed that."

"Is that for whom you are crying?" Enoch touches her hand. "We have a funny relationship with pain, don't we? I suppose we all enjoy a little pain now and then. Provided the pain has a precise time at which it starts and ends. Like a strenuous hike through the canyon. Or a roller coaster ride. But pain without parameters? Like heartbreak? Or grief at the loss of a loved one? Well, that's the kind of pain that doesn't start and end at our convenience. I don't think the IMPs were designed to alleviate suffering, but that's what people use them for. Hard to believe, but there was a time when we had no choice but to cope with our anguish. I suppose the art of growing old is training your soul to manage all the accumulated pain."

Maggie's mind turns to the other members of her bible study group. Perhaps right now, at that very moment, they are having adventures of their own, each with an IMP projecting a different version of Juliana Deepmere, each seeking an answer to an urgent question. The problem, as Maggie sees it, is that any solution the IMP may propose will invariably lead to more questions, and at some point, the answers will begin to contradict one another. An answer from an IMP can seem absolute, immutable, permanent, but impermanence is built into the fabric of reality. There's no getting around it. She can see that now.

Enoch shrugs and smiles.

"I'm tempted to say I'm speaking to an illusion right now. But then, who knows? Maybe I'm the one who's an illusion. Or maybe life itself is one big illusion. Some people believe that you know. The Travelers certainly do. It's one of their philosophical tenets. Life, they say, is a marvelous dream. No IMPs required. But the final answer to this great mystery will remain forever hidden."

Ticket Off-Planet

EDITOR'S NOTE: What follows are several handwritten pages stapled to the final pass of the uncorrected manuscript. Since the author, a notorious recluse who has gone off the grid, could not be contacted about his intentions, the editorial board has elected to print the pages in their entirety with slight modifications for clarity.

This book came to me, all at once, in a dream.

Some months ago, while visiting my daughter at Cambridge, I strolled one Yuletide evening through the snowy lanes and, feeling festive, wandered into a teashop where I ran into an old acquaintance who invited me to join him and his friends at a table near a frosted window offering an impressive view of the School of Pythagoras. Before engaging in the obligatory chit-chat ("What brings you to merry old England?" "I've forgotten that you take your tea black"), Rupert ladled a heaping spoon of sugar into his cup of Darjeeling and launched into a speech about an underground organization that he and his friends had founded. Such a revelation hardly shocked me. Rupert, you must understand, was an eccentric fellow. An accomplished biochemist, a connoisseur of human souls, and a brewmaster of some renown, he had dedicated much of his career to what philosophers call "the hard problem of consciousness."

Considered a pseudoscientific heretic by his dogmatic colleagues, Rupert believed the physical brain had little to do with the experience of being, and no amount of neural mapping could adequately explain how a three-pound piece of meat locked inside a skull could produce the taste of chocolate and the stirring sounds of a Beethoven string quartet.

"The scientific paradigm," he insisted, "isn't merely missing a crucial piece of information that, once discovered, will finally explain how unconscious matter produces consciousness. Science, as currently practiced, has led us into an intellectual cul-de-sac. An entirely different approach is needed. We, that is, Terrence, Bernardo, Donald, Aldous, and I, believe mind, not matter, is the fundamental stuff of which the universe is made. To help us better understand the ultimate source of being, the five of us gather here once a month and take a heroic dose of THC. 100 milligrams usually does the trick. We then visit the Cathedral of Saint Blaise to listen to evensong and meditate. We find that proximity to the sacred is of utmost importance. A laboratory setting would never do. Nevertheless, we regard the cathedral as a technological wonder. A medieval spaceship. An edifice intentionally designed to lift the human spirit from the confines of the limited ego into an ineffable transcendent realm. Rather than an experiment in the formal sense of the word, Cathedrals on Cannabis has become an ongoing series of adventures in consciousness."

Fascinated, I asked if I might join them that evening on their "adventure." An ecumenical and open-minded bunch, the caffeinated quintet was delighted to initiate me as the club's newest member. Casting a surreptitious glance around the teashop, Rupert reached into his leather satchel and handed me a small, yellow lozenge. One hour prior to evensong, we placed the drug on our tongues (tart, lemony, with a slightly bitter finish) and then walked to the steps of Saint Blaise.

"Now is the time, depending on your personal beliefs, to invoke a spiritual guide or a more-than-human consciousness that will help you on your journey."

I should probably pause to say that, having rejected the faith of my fathers, I no longer believed in a supernatural order and considered myself an acolyte of the New Atheist movement. I was also something of a teetotaler and had only dabbled in psychoactive drugs during my hazy undergraduate days. Still, I was curious to find out what I might *experience, but before I could enter the cathedral, Rupert explained how new members, while waiting for the effects of the THC to kick in, must first "make a miniature pilgrimage" by slowly circumambulating the cathedral.*

At twilight, as a full moon floated above the cathedral and my mind was beginning to drift, we lowered our heads and, in silence, circled the building. Although it was a bit blustery, I had dressed for the occasion and enjoyed the crisp December air blowing against my face. I couldn't say how many laps we made. I only knew that my mind was getting foggier by the minute. At some point, Rupert tapped me on the shoulder. We climbed the stairs and passed under the imposing arched entranceway. Inside, pale light filtered through the stained-glass windows and fell in thin blue pools in the transept. The walls of rough-hewn stone towered on either side of us like granite cliffs. We took a pew at the center of the nave, the best spot to appreciate the spacious acoustics and magnificent flying buttresses rising to a midnight blue ceiling studded with white stars.

While the others closed their eyes and concentrated on the chorus, I studied the devotional sculpture situated under the gilded dome of the apse. In her arms, the Virgin held the broken body of her dead son. I gazed at the gaping holes in the man's feet and the inconsolable expression on the woman's face. Though I had never been inside this "medieval spaceship" and had yet to familiarize myself with its storied history, I knew somehow that the painted wood from which the figures were carved came from a walnut tree felled nearly one thousand years ago in the north country. I could see it clearly in my mind: a deep forest of Douglas fir and mighty hemlock. My mind began making even stranger associations. For some reason, I believed my new friends and I made our den there but had left the forest tonight to find better hunting grounds.

Before arriving at the cathedral, we trotted in single file along a wooded ridge overlooking hills and dales. One by one, we weaved down an icy switchback and, for the next five miles, traveled across the deforested landscape. There were few trees to shield us from the brutal winter gusts, no rock ledges and caves where we might take shelter from the pelting snow. To the blare of horns and roar of diesel engines, we darted over an eight-lane motorway. Somehow, all six of us survived the perilous crossing.

At an underpass littered with shattered bottles and flattened aluminum cans, we listened for the telltale scuttle of sewer rats that had left shallow prints in the snow. Between two warehouses, a fierce wind whipped up a flurry of blue plastic bags. We kept moving. One mile later, we saw the silhouette of a lift bridge against the cold, gray sky and a jumble of stone cottages perched precariously on the slopes of a river valley. Here, the snow became patchy and uneven, and a fine sodium-tinged ash coated a set of railroad tracks that vanished into shadow.

Our ears involuntarily pricked up. A solitary doe, separated from the herd, jumped from the brambles onto the frozen river. In a panic, it skittered along the ice. We moved quickly, the six of us giving chase, and managed to take down the doe. We dragged the carcass, wet and steaming with blood, back to the embankment and, for the first time in days, fed on the flesh of a fresh kill. Yapping and whining, we darted excitedly around the body.

Upriver, a mournful horn called in the night. The ice began to groan and shift with slow seismic certainty. We leaped away from the embankment as the ice splintered and then exploded. Moments later, an iron ore ship, navigating the treacherous oxbow bend, cast a blinding beam of white light across the icy monoliths. Taking cover behind a mountain of river rock, we watched helplessly as our kill was swept away by the shifting ice. We did not howl or whine. Instead, we licked with relish the blood already freezing to our filthy pelts and then climbed the embankment.

In the orange glow of city lights, we slunk through a chaos of crooked lanes. We passed a squat brick schoolhouse and a bus shelter reeking of urine. From a tangle of clotheslines, an invisible bird cawed mockingly at us. Across the street from a mean, windowless public house, we watched men scowl and curse as they stumbled out the door into the frozen waste. *The neighborhood abounded with pigeons, possums, raccoons, feral cats, and small yapping dogs. Fertile feeding grounds. We ate to our heart's content.*

But now, through the icy streets, there marched a bearded man in baggy fatigues. An expert shot hired by the mayor to exterminate cave dwellers like us, the man smelled almost as wild as the animals he tracked. Meticulous in his work, he knelt in the snow to study our prints and droppings and the tufts of coarse, brindled hair wedged between the slats of busted fences. Once he established the number in our pack, he laid his trap. For bait, he used roadkill, placing the carcass of a squirrel under an oak. From his perch on an uncertain limb, he patiently waited for us to feed. He managed to get Rupert first. Then the others.

I darted down a distant alley, the sole survivor, and watched my brothers writhe in agony before going still. I crept through the surrounding terrain, slinking by a cannery and peering through the basement windows of a Russian bathhouse that had been in continuous operation since it first opened its doors during the days when Stanisław Lem came to town on a reading tour. I stood before the colossal wreck of a warehouse, its chimney protruding like an obscene finger from the vacant lots all around. Many years ago, books were printed and packaged here and then shipped to locations around the globe. A young woman with wild red hair coaxed me inside with a stale biscuit.

Filled with the rusted levers and gears of enormous, antiquated machines, the warehouse now served as home to a dozen or so artists who'd unlawfully set up their studios here. I wandered freely through the woman's enormous loft, ignoring the cloying chemical odors and clouds of cigarette smoke. I played with the stuffed animals and squeaky toys she gave me. She went to a kitchenette and cracked open a can of dog food. Though she looked desperate enough to eat some of the gelatinous chow herself, she scooped the contents into a bowl and placed it in front of me. In a dark corner, using a heap of tattered towels, she built me a cozy bed.

In the feeble lamplight, I observed her stitching together huge hunks of tawny rawhide to create the strange, twisted architectures of an imaginary city. She seemed to be at her most productive, her most wildly creative, in the early hours before dawn. Whenever she paused to smoke a little grass or take a pull from a nearby bottle, she sat beside me and scratched behind my ears. She praised me, stroking my back, and told me how she respected my animal nature. "For the whole of nature, both good and evil, has an important role in the creation of new things." Untroubled by the loud music and maniacal laughter that echoed continually through the empty corridors and stairwells, I felt my eyes growing heavy and slept in snatches.

The following morning, my belly bloated, I boldly trotted in broad daylight down a busy boulevard. On a residential street of weather-beaten bungalows, I foraged for food in an overturned trashcan. As I pulled a putrid T-bone from a plastic bag, I heard an unusual sound. I sidled into a garden and, to my delight, discovered a makeshift coop made of plywood and a corrugated tin roof. Behind a stretch of poorly maintained chicken wire, a fat hen and five chicks scratched mindlessly at the snow and pecked at the seeds scattered around the coop. It took only a matter of minutes for me to gnaw a hole in the wire and slaughter all six fowl. I darted back and forth through a blizzard of bloody feathers. In my frenzy, I barely felt the hot sting of the bullet. It ripped right through my body and penetrated the plywood walls of the chicken coop. The man, hiding on a high limb of a craggy elm, shifted his elbow and adjusted his scope.

I bolted, leaping over the fence, and disappeared down a cobblestone lane.

On the town's outskirts, I rested in an abandoned house. Nothing disturbed my sleep until I felt the floorboards shivering and heard a glass pane crash to the floor. On the street, a crew in hard hats and orange vests gave the signal. Without bothering to inspect the house for the drunks and junkies who, judging from the scent, regularly took shelter there, the crane operator swung the boom and dropped the wrecking ball straight through the roof. Barely able to muster the strength, I rolled through the back doorway and hobbled across the yard.

At dusk, I limped toward the sanctuary of Saint Blaise. After investigating a hole at the bottom of a smashed and splintered door behind the sacristy, I lowered my head and, like a wounded soldier returning from the frontlines of war, dragged myself down the center aisle. The midwinter wind battered the steeple, and the buttresses creaked like a ship in heavy seas. Moonlight shone through the stained-glass windows, and the cathedral glowed an incandescent green that reminded me of how I once roamed freely in the forest. I paced back and forth before the pieta before making a bed in a pile of embroidered linens and dusty hymnals. Blood bubbled from my gut. My breathing became irregular, and my dark eyes became distant and unfocused. I looked up at the ornately carved statue but did not see the tortured faces of the mother and son. Instead, I saw only the ancient tree from which the statue had been carved.

At the west entrance, one of the doors scraped against the cracked marble floor. Though I struggled to raise my head, I detected the approaching figure of the bearded man. In a final effort to intimidate my foe, I growled and flashed my teeth. The man stopped beside the sanctified sculpture and, before taking aim, said something about the patron saint of animals. I rested my head against the sculpture's pedestal and gave a heavy sigh.

The rifle shot erupted like an organ blast through the cathedral.

Then I opened my eyes — and found myself sitting again in a pew beside Rupert, listening to the angelic strains of evensong.

Early the next morning, I began writing this book.

Here are my final corrections. I think you'll find them an improvement over previous versions. Wishing you continued success in this fickle industry and hoping you find your very own ticket off-planet one day soon.

Your Fellow Traveler,
Kevin

About the Author

After working as a boilermaker in the steel mills in Ohio, KEVIN P. KEATING became an instructor of English and began teaching at Baldwin Wallace University, John Carroll University, and Kent State University. His essays and stories have appeared in nearly one hundred literary journals. His first novel *The Natural Order of Things* (Vintage Contemporaries) was a finalist for the *Los Angeles Times* Books Prize/First Fiction Award. His second novel *The Captive Condition* (Pantheon) was launched at the San Diego Comic-Con. Both novels received starred reviews from *Publishers Weekly*. He is the recipient of a Creative Workforce Fellowship, the Cleveland Arts Prize, the James Thurber House Writer-in-Residence Award, and many other distinctions. He currently resides in Cleveland, Ohio.

IFF
BOOKS

ACADEMIC AND SPECIALIST

Iff Books publishes non-fiction. It aims to work with authors and
titles that augment our understanding of the human condition,
society and civilisation, and the world or universe in which we live.
If you have enjoyed this book, why not tell other readers by
posting a review on your preferred book site.
Recent bestsellers from Iff Books are:

Why Materialism Is Baloney
How true skeptics know there is no death and fathom answers
to life, the universe, and everything
Bernardo Kastrup
A hard-nosed, logical, and skeptic non-materialist metaphysics,
according to which the body is in mind, not mind in the body.
Paperback: 978-1-78279-362-5 ebook: 978-1-78279-361-8

The Fall
Steve Taylor
The Fall discusses human achievement versus the issues of war,
patriarchy and social inequality.
Paperback: 978-1-78535-804-3 ebook: 978-1-78535-805-0

Brief Peeks Beyond
Critical essays on metaphysics, neuroscience, free will,
skepticism and culture
Bernardo Kastrup
An incisive, original, compelling alternative to current mainstream
cultural views and assumptions.
Paperback: 978-1-78535-018-4 ebook: 978-1-78535-019-1

Framespotting
Changing how you look at things changes how
you see them
Laurence & Alison Matthews
A punchy, upbeat guide to framespotting. Spot deceptions and
hidden assumptions; swap growth for growing up. See and be free.
Paperback: 978-1-78279-689-3 ebook: 978-1-78279-822-4

Is There an Afterlife?
David Fontana
Is there an Afterlife? If so what is it like? How do Western ideas
of the afterlife compare with Eastern? David Fontana presents the
historical and contemporary evidence for survival of
physical death.
Paperback: 978-1-90381-690-5

Nothing Matters
a book about nothing
Ronald Green
Thinking about Nothing opens the world to everything by
illuminating new angles to old problems and stimulating new
ways of thinking.
Paperback: 978-1-84694-707-0 ebook: 978-1-78099-016-3

Panpsychism
The Philosophy of the Sensuous Cosmos
Peter Ells
Are free will and mind chimeras? This book, anti-materialistic but
respecting science, answers: No! Mind is foundational
to all existence.
Paperback: 978-1-84694-505-2 ebook: 978-1-78099-018-7

Punk Science
Inside the Mind of God
Manjir Samanta-Laughton
Many have experienced unexplainable phenomena; God, psychic
abilities, extraordinary healing and angelic encounters. Can
cutting-edge science actually explain phenomena
previously thought of as 'paranormal'?
Paperback: 978-1-90504-793-2

The Vagabond Spirit of Poetry
Edward Clarke
Spend time with the wisest poets of the modern age and of the
past, and let Edward Clarke remind you of the importance of
poetry in our industrialized world.
Paperback: 978-1-78279-370-0 ebook: 978-1-78279-369-4

Readers of ebooks can buy or view any of these bestsellers by
clicking on the live link in the title. Most titles are published in
paperback and as an ebook. Paperbacks are available in traditional
bookshops. Both print and ebook formats are available online.
Find more titles and sign up to our readers' newsletter at
www.collectiveinkbooks.com/non-fiction
Follow us on Facebook at
www.facebook.com/CINonFiction